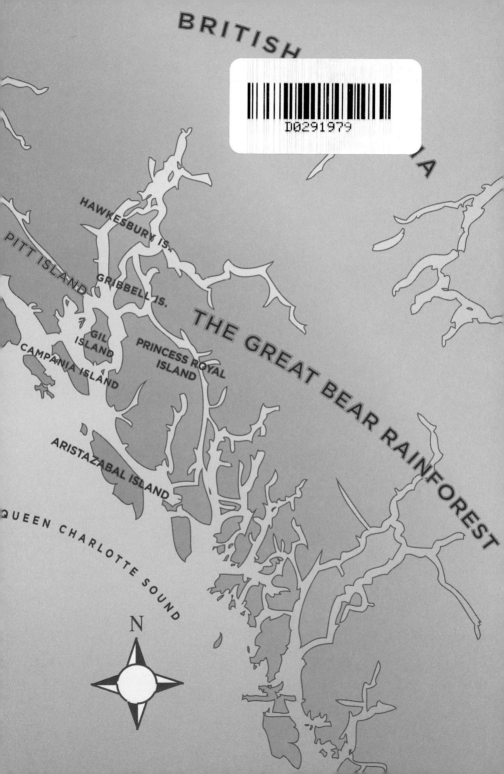

BRITISH

IA

HAWKESBURY IS.

PITT ISLAND

GRIBBELL IS.

THE GREAT BEAR RAINFOREST

GIL
ISLAND

PRINCESS ROYAL
ISLAND

CAMPANIA ISLAND

ARISTAZABAL ISLAND

QUEEN CHARLOTTE SOUND

N

TRAVELS WITH GANNON & WYATT

GREAT BEAR
RAINFOREST

PATTI WHEELER & KEITH HEMSTREET

GREENLEAF
BOOK GROUP PRESS

Published by Greenleaf Book Group Press
Austin, Texas
www.gbgpress.com

Distributed by Greenleaf Book Group LLC

For ordering information or special discounts for bulk purchases, please contact Greenleaf Book Group LLC at PO Box 91869, Austin, TX 78709, 512.891.6100.

Design and composition by Greenleaf Book Group LLC
Cover design by Leon Godwin & Greenleaf Book Group LLC
Cover illustration by Leon Godwin
interior bear claw print image©iStockphoto.com/scamartini

Publisher's Cataloging-In-Publication Data
(Prepared by The Donohue Group, Inc.)

Wheeler, Patti.
    Travels with Gannon & Wyatt. Great Bear Rainforest / Patti Wheeler & Keith Hemstreet. -- 1st ed.
    p. : ill. ; cm.
    Summary: Gannon and Wyatt join an expedition into the Great Bear Rainforest in search of the mythical spirit bear, but when members of the expedition go missing, the brothers bravely set out on a search-and-rescue mission. As they find themselves lost in a dangerous forest, they are guided by the wisdom of the First Nation people and uncover a sinister plot. The brothers must risk everything to save those who are missing and restore balance to the Great Bear. Based on real-life brothers, this series is supported by video, photos, and more stories found online at travelswithgannonandwyatt.com.
    Interest age level: 009-012.
    Issued also as an ebook.
    ISBN: 978-1-60832-588-7

    1. Twins—Juvenile fiction. 2. Missing persons—British Columbia—Great Bear Rainforest—Juvenile fiction. 3. Bears—British Columbia—Great Bear Rainforest—Juvenile fiction. 4. Indians of North America—British Columbia—Great Bear Rainforest—Juvenile fiction. 5. Adventure and adventurers—British Columbia—Great Bear Rainforest—Juvenile fiction. 6. Great Bear Rainforest (B.C.)—uvenile fiction. 7. Twins—Fiction. 8. Missing persons—British Columbia—Great Bear Rainforest—Fiction. 9. Bears—British Columbia—Great Bear Rainforest—Fiction. 10. Indians of North America—British Columbia—Great Bear Rainforest—Fiction. 11. Adventure and adventurers—British Columbia—Great Bear Rainforest—Fiction. 12. Great Bear Rainforest (B.C.)—Fiction. 13. Adventure stories. 14. Diary fiction. I. Hemstreet, Keith. II. Title. III. Title: Travels with Gannon and Wyatt. IV. Title: Great Bear Rainforest
PZ7.W5663 Gre 2013
[Fic]   2013933154

Part of the Tree Neutral® program, which offsets the number of trees consumed in the production and printing of this book by taking proactive steps, such as planting trees in direct proportion to the number of trees used: www.treeneutral.com

Printed in the United States of America on acid-free paper

13 14 15 16 17 18   10 9 8 7 6 5 4 3 2 1

First Edition

TreeNeutral®

Conservation is a state of harmony
between men and land.
—Aldo Leopold

For we do not own this land so much as the land owns us.
The land is part of us, and we are part of the land.
—Haisla Nation: The Kitlope Declaration

ENGLISH/GITGA'TT:
TRANSLATION OF COMMON PHRASES

How are you?—Nda wila waalu?

I am fine—Aam wila waalu.

What is your name?—Naayu di waan?

My name is . . . — di waayu . . .

Where are you from?—Ndaayu di wil waatgn?

Thank you, sir/madam—Tooyxsut nuun

I'm hungry—Kwdiinu

I'm thirsty—Luguungwaga'nu

I like—Anoogi

I don't like—Akadi anooxt/anoogu

I want—Hasagu

I do not want—Akadi hasagu

Where is . . . —Ndaayut?

CONTENTS

PART I

ITCHING TO GO SOMEWHERE

GANNON

Okay, here we go again, but before I get into the adventure at hand and put down in my journal how the whole thing was set in motion, I want to take a minute to get something off my mind, which is basically this: I'm totally flabbergasted by what's expected of kids these days!

I mean, between school, sports, chores, and all of the other things that consume our lives, we hardly have time to stop and smell the roses. My parents tell me that learning to handle all of these responsibilities is just part of "growing up," part of becoming a "well-rounded individual," that dealing with these obligations, and I'm quoting my parents here, "helps build character and instill a good work ethic."

Well, fine. Whatever. Some of that may be true, but it sure as heck doesn't make it any easier.

When the captain called yesterday, I was feeling totally overwhelmed because of all the stuff I had to do and almost none of it, I was pretty sure, would help make me a more "well-rounded individual." First, there was my room, which had become a total mess after days of neglect with dirty clothes all over the place and a couple overflowing garbage cans and mud on the carpet that I'd tracked in after my last hike. To make matters worse, it was my day to do the dishes, mop up the floors, and take out the trash. So I had all this stuff weighing on me, not to mention all the undone schoolwork piling up on my desk that I won't even bother to talk about.

Now, I'm not one to shun my chores. Okay, fine. I am. But I have a good excuse, which is . . . well . . . oh, who am I kidding? I don't have an excuse. Chores just bug me. Period. The end.

Now, where was I? Oh, yeah. Procrastinating. An art I've nearly perfected. So, there I was kicked back on the couch trying to think of ways to get myself out of all these chores, when the phone rang.

I picked it up and said, "hello."

"Hello there, Gannon!" came a booming Irish voice.

"Captain Colin?" I asked. "Is that you?"

"You bet it is!"

Captain Colin is an old friend my parents met at a pub in Dublin, Ireland, sometime before my brother and I were born. Story goes, they stayed in the pub singing Irish ballads until the sun came up and got along so well that the captain invited them on a weekend sailing trip to the Isle of Man. Needless to say, they accepted, more rowdiness ensued, and details of the adventure become pretty vague after that, I'm guessing for good reason. Anyway, they've been good chums ever since.

"It's great to hear your voice, Captain!" I said.

"Good to hears yours, too, lad!"

Captain Colin told me that he and the crew of the Pacific Yellowfin were taking some famous environmental scientist I'd never heard of into the Great Bear Rainforest to study the habitat of the *spirit bear*, and after all that was done they were going to volunteer at a whale research lab where the scientists needed help repairing a station that had been damaged during a severe storm.

"That all sounds pretty cool, Captain," I said.

Then he told me the best part.

"We have two empty rooms aboard the boat," he said. "That is, unless your family cares to fill them."

It didn't take me two seconds to answer. I mean, of course we wanted to fill them! We're talking about a trip to the Great Bear Rainforest! Who in the world would say no to that?

"Here's the catch," Captain Colin said. "We depart in forty-eight hours. Can you make it on such short notice?"

Forty-eight hours! That meant we'd have to start preparing for the trip right away, and if that were the case, I'd have a totally legitimate excuse to blow off my chores.

"I really hope we can," I said to the captain. "But, let me check with my dad."

I yelled at the top of my lungs.

"Dad, can we go to the Great Bear Rainforest?"

My dad strolled around the corner into the room, a cup of coffee in his hand.

"Can we go where?" he asked.

"To the Great Bear Rainforest! Captain Colin has room aboard the Pacific Yellowfin! Can we go? Come on! Please!"

"Well, that's very kind of him to invite us. I suppose I could do some work while we were there. Paintings of the rainforest would actually be a wonderful addition to my museum exhibit this winter."

"A *wonderful* addition," I said, agreeing enthusiastically.

"And I know how much your mom loves boating."

"Are you kidding? She flips over it!"

"When would we leave?" my dad asked as he took another sip.

"In forty-eight hours."

My dad gasped, nearly choking on his coffee.

"I'll take that as a yes," I said and returned to the phone.

"Thank you for thinking of us, Captain," I said. "You couldn't have called at a better time."

"Don't mention it," he said. "When I realized we would have extra rooms on the boat, you were the first people that came to mind. I know how much your family enjoys exploring new places. So, what do you say? You on board?"

"We're definitely on board."

I walked over and smacked my dad on the back a few times, as he continued to cough up the coffee that he had sucked down his windpipe.

"You're going to love this place," the captain said. "It's truly magical."

"I bet it is."

"Listen, I have to go ashore to take care of some business. Do you have any questions before I go?"

"I have two, actually."

"I'm all ears, laddy."

"Where in the world is this place, and what on earth is a spirit bear?"

The captain broke into a hearty laugh.

And so it happened that we were invited to join Captain Colin's expedition into the Great Bear Rainforest.

Okay, then, that's enough for now. Time to pack.

WYATT
SEPTEMBER 17, 11:42 AM
ABOARD FLIGHT 417 DENVER, COLORADO
TO VANCOUVER, B.C.

The FIRST LAW OF EXPLORATION is to know your destination. This may seem impossible in some respects, as the nature of exploration is to set off into the unknown, but these days you can find information on just about every place on earth—books written by notable people, travel essays, photos, documentaries, maps, etc. The information is out there. Find it. Read it. Know it.

I usually abide by this law wholeheartedly, but I just learned of this trip yesterday and we're already on the plane en route to Canada. So I didn't have a whole lot of time to study before we left. The only thing I really know about the area is that it was first explored by Captain George Vancouver—a protégé of the famous Captain James Cook—who in the late 1700s mapped much of the coastline and got a beautiful city named after him for his effort. I guess on this adventure I'll just have to learn on the fly. Actually, my grade will depend on it. The fall semester of home schooling is under way and we're studying unique ecosystems. I was going to do a report on the Amazon Jungle, a tropical rainforest in South America, but after learning of our trip, I obviously wanted to change the subject of my report to the Great Bear Rainforest, a temperate rainforest in North America.

When we got the call from Captain Colin, my mom was working as a flight attendant on the London-Denver route for World Airlines. Luckily, I got in touch with her between flights to discuss the report. Turns out, she had already spoken to the captain.

"Of course you can do your report on the Great Bear," she said over the phone. "I was going to suggest it myself. Besides, we'll visit the Amazon eventually. It's a place I've always wanted to see."

"Sounds good, Mom. Thanks."

"When I spoke with Captain Colin, he said there's going to be an environmental scientist aboard the boat."

"Really?" I said. "Gannon didn't mention anything about it. Do you know who it is?"

"I think his name is Brezner something or other."

"It wouldn't be Dr. Hans Brezner, would it?"

"Yes, I think that's it."

"Are you kidding me?" I shouted.

"No, why? Have you heard of him?"

"Have I heard of him? He was one of the most important environmental scientists in the world!"

"Was?"

"He's dedicated his life to protecting some of the earth's most pristine environments, but a few years back he lost a battle to preserve a large area of Patagonia and he's pretty much been off the radar ever since."

"Well, the two of you will have plenty of time to get to know each other while we're aboard the boat. Personally, I can't wait to volunteer at the whale research lab. That will be a great learning experience for all of us."

"This is going to be an incredible trip!"

"I'll meet you in Vancouver tomorrow afternoon. Dad has my flight information."

"Sounds like a plan."

As an artist, my dad was thrilled by the idea of creating a series of paintings set in the Great Bear Rainforest. What really had him excited was the opportunity to photograph and paint a spirit bear. A spirit bear is a black bear with a

9

rare genetic mutation that causes it to be white. This will definitely require some luck, as very few people ever actually see one.

My dad was all wound up and went on and on about the paints he would use and the colors he would mix and how he would display the canvases at his winter exhibit. Eventually, I stopped listening. My interest is not in art. It's in science.

Recently, my brother and I had received a letter from the Youth Exploration Society, thanking us for the reports we had provided on the environment of the Kalahari Desert and Okavango Delta of Botswana.

"The field notes you submitted make for a wonderful addition to our library," the letter read. "Your thoroughness and attention to detail provide a valuable documentation of this unique region of Africa, and for that, the Youth Exploration Society is grateful."

Receiving such a letter from one of the world's foremost authorities on exploration was certainly a boost to the ego. So much so, I was already anxious to send in my next set of field notes. This trip would give me a chance to do just that.

Even more exciting, this trip would allow me to meet and study with a scientist who was at one time considered the best in his field. And to do it in a place like the Great Bear Rainforest, well, to an aspiring scientist, that's better than winning the lottery.

GANNON
SEPTEMBER 18
VANCOUVER, BRITISH COLUMBIA

Immigration . . . Vancouver, Canada

Okay, we've made it to Canada, our fine neighbor to the north. Right now we're sitting in the Vancouver International Airport waiting for a shuttle or taxi or something to take us to a floatplane that will fly us to the Great Bear. Here's the thing about traveling to another country, even a place as friendly as Canada: they don't just roll out the welcome mat when you get there. At least, not right away. There's always the process of getting approved by some kind of border patrol, which, for someone like me who likes to joke around, can go good or bad, depending.

I'd be willing to bet my last dollar that they teach "intimidation" to all border agents. Get tied up with an especially curious agent and you could wind up answering questions for about a day and a half, give or take. Sounds simple enough, answering questions, but it's not and here's why: when you answer a border patrol's questions, they stare at you as if you're lying to their face. I mean, they're so good at what they do they can make you feel guilty of a crime you never committed. Below is an example. Okay, I made it up, but it's very realistic.

BORDER AGENT: How are you today?
ME: Good.
The agent stares at me, disbelief in his eyes.
ME: Pretty good.
The agent stares even harder. A drop of sweat runs down my forehead.

ME: Truth is, I could be better.

BORDER AGENT: Are you bringing anything illegal into this country?

ME: No.

BORDER AGENT: Are you sure?

ME: No . . . I mean, yes. I mean, I don't know . . .

BORDER AGENT: Detain this boy at once!

I guess it's understandable. After all, they are the first line of defense and their job is to protect their country by keeping the bad people out and that's pretty important stuff, so, of course they are going to be serious about what they do, but I'd much rather be playful than serious and in this sort of situation that can have good or bad results, as I said.

Walking up to the agent at the Immigration and Customs desk, I suddenly remembered a Canadian movie where the actors kept saying "eh" at the end of almost every sentence and that just cracked me up, so I figured talking "Canadian" would be as good a way as any to break the ice.

"How's it going, eh?" I said.

Turns out, it wasn't such a good idea. Given the way the agent stared at me without saying a word, it was obvious he didn't find it very amusing. Apparently, not all Canadians speak that way.

"Are you visiting for business or pleasure?" he finally asked.

"Pleasure," I said.

"And research," Wyatt added. "We're going to view the wildlife in the Great Bear Rainforest."

"Brave young men," the agent said.

He leaned over the counter and looked us in the eyes.

"I have some advice," he whispered.

"We're all ears," I said.

"Try not to get mauled by a grizzly or torn to pieces by a pack of wolves."

Wyatt and I looked at each other, our eyes wide with fear.

"Yeah, we'll do our best," Wyatt said.

The agent winked as he stamped our passports.

"Thanks for the advice," I said.

"No problem . . . eh."

WYATT

SEPTEMBER 18, 2:51 PM
VANCOUVER, B.C.
23° CELSIUS, 73° FAHRENHEIT
MOSTLY SUNNY, WIND CALM

After clearing customs and immigration in Vancouver, a van took us to a marina on the northeast side of the city. From the docks, I looked to the sky and spotted a small aircraft flying over the mountains. On the bottom of the plane, where you normally find wheels, were two large pontoons. They looked a lot like big water skis. The plane flew in low and touched down, skipping a few times across the water's choppy surface before settling. The pilot passed the dock and made a quick

U-turn. As the plane drifted toward us, the propeller slowed and came to a stop.

The seaplane that flew us to the GBR

The door swung open and the pilot stuck his head outside. His shirt was unbuttoned below his chest and his brown hair was shaggy and disheveled, as if he'd just rolled out of bed. He was wearing flip-flops.

"You the group that's headed up to Bella Bella?" the pilot asked.

"That's us," my dad said.

"Excellent. I'm Brad. I'll be your pilot today."

Brad threw us a rope and we secured the plane to the dock.

"Hop aboard!" he said.

As usual, my mom was nervous about getting on a small aircraft and went about interrogating the pilot.

"How old is this plane, Brad?" she asked, sternly.

"It's an A185F floatplane, ma'am," Brad answered, cordially. "Built in 1976."

"How frequently do you service the engine?"

"Whenever service is needed."

"Is it needed often?"

"Not really."

"How do you know when it's needed?"

"I just know."

Judging by the look on my mom's face, I thought she was about to cancel the trip all together. As a seasoned flight attendant, she's logged more flying time than most people. She has no problem with jumbo jets, but small planes have always spooked her. Sensing her unease, Brad attempted to calm her nerves.

"Don't you worry, ma'am," he said, "This plane is old, but she runs as good as new."

Brad's reassurance wasn't enough. The grilling continued.

"Where is your co-pilot?"

"Ma'am," he replied. "It's just me."

She turned to us.

"What if something happens to Brad during the flight?" she whispered.

"Like what?" my dad asked.

"Like he gets sick or passes out or has a heart attack? We'll crash!"

"He's not that old. I doubt he'll have a heart attack."

"You never know."

She turned to Brad.

"Brad," she said, "how's your heart?"

"My heart?" he asked.

"Yes, your heart."

Brad put his hand over his chest.

"Still beating, as far as I can tell."

It's true, pilots along the western coast of British Columbia have a long and spectacular history of crashing. But, it's not because they have heart attacks. Mostly, it's due to weather. The storms in this area are frequent and can be fierce, making the conditions for air travel less than ideal. But today in Vancouver, there wasn't a storm cloud in the sky.

"It's a perfect day to fly, Mom," I said and hopped aboard, leaving my dad to further convince her that it was safe. It took a few minutes, but my dad was finally able to coax her onto the plane.

Brad fired up the engine and put on his headset. After idling into the channel, he turned to us.

"Everyone buckled?" he asked.

We all gave the thumbs up.

"Good! Off we go!"

Brad pressed the throttle forward and we quickly gained momentum. The pontoons thumped hard atop the rough waters, rattling the plane like an earthquake. Then, suddenly, the earthquake was over. We were airborne.

It's been smooth sailing ever since.

Time to put away the journal and enjoy the scenery . . .

Aerial view of the GBR

GANNON
MID-FLIGHT

Wow, what a view! Spread out a few thousand feet below us is the southern boundary of the Great Bear Rainforest—a huge mountainous wilderness carved up by channels and inlets and tributaries and spotted with hundreds of lakes and dozens of small, tree-covered islands. Further inland there are mountains so high trees can't even grow and between many of these high jagged peaks, gray and white glaciers snake their way into the valleys.

It's really kind of mind-blowing to think that hidden somewhere within this coastal wilderness, somewhere underneath the water and the trees, are some of the world's most impressive creatures—humpback and orca whales, stellar sea lions, grizzlies, black bears, wolves, moose, bald eagles, and hundreds of other species. It's even more amazing to think that somewhere in that forest down there is the mythical spirit bear!

WYATT
SEPTEMBER 18, 3:23 PM
FLOATPLANE, APPROACHING BELLA BELLA, B.C.
CLOUDY SKIES

Below us right now is a section of land that has almost no trees, just lots of stumps and fallen trunks. In such a lush forest, it looks like a terrible scar on the earth.

I guess this remote wilderness isn't as "undisturbed" as I thought. I can see a crane on one side loading a massive truck with trees. It's obviously a logging operation. Through my binoculars I can see the name "Halliman Timber" printed on the crane.

Witnessing this makes it pretty clear to me why some

people devote their lives to saving the earth's forests. I under-stand that timber is needed. We use it to build homes. We use it for fuel. It's a valuable resource. I just have a hard time believing there isn't a way to protect the world's last old growth forests from clear-cutting, and still address the needs of humans.

An old growth forest being clear-cut

GANNON
BELLA BELLA

Brad got us to Bella Bella after about an hour-long flight and I have to compliment him on his landing. I mean, it was perfect, with the plane touching down in the inlet as smooth as a pelican gliding onto water. From there he steered us to an old, decaying dock near the village, and now we're just waiting for a ride to the Pacific Yellowfin, which is anchored in a deep bay a few minutes away.

According to Brad, about 1,400 people live in Bella Bella, mostly descendants of the native tribe, Heiltsuk. Apartment buildings and small homes line the shore. Just about everyone has a satellite dish and almost all of the buildings are painted sky blue or white, probably to give some kind of color to a place that sits under gray skies for most of the year.

I see a little center consol boat speeding toward us from across the inlet. I'm guessing this is our ride.

More later . . .

WYATT

4:32 PM
BELLA BELLA, B.C.
14° CELSIUS, 57° FAHRENHEIT
CLOUDY SKIES, WIND 10-15 MPH

As we raced toward the bay in the water taxi, a mist blew through the air and I could taste the ocean on my lips. Rounding a small island, the ship came into view. The Pacific Yellowfin, our home for the next ten days!

Captain Colin and the crew were gathered on the starboard bow, awaiting our arrival.

"Welcome, explorers!" Captain Colin hollered as we neared the ship. "Climb aboard! The Great Bear awaits!"

The Pacific Yellowfin awaiting our arrival

Wearing a pressed black oxford shirt with captain stripes proudly displayed over his broad shoulders, Captain Colin O'Brien is a respectable figure. First off, he's tall, about six feet, two inches, with red hair and fair, freckled skin. Second, he has this thunderous voice that makes him sound very confident in all that he says. Third, he's worked on boats longer than I've been alive. In over a quarter century as a ship captain, he has navigated almost every ocean on the planet. It's the northwest coast of British Columbia, however, that he decided to make his home. This is a place, he said, that captures his imagination more than any other.

In addition to Captain Colin are two other men with over fifty years of experience between them. "Salty" Joe Bollock, first mate and cook, and Liam Glasgow, chief engineer and self-proclaimed "man who can fix anything, anytime, anywhere."

Salty Joe has the look of a hardened seaman with a prickly white crew cut and weathered skin. Short and stocky, his eyes are narrow slits, his face has deep lines, and he speaks out of the left side of his mouth. Basically, he looks like an old pirate. Joe took his first job aboard a crab boat at the age of fifteen, thirty-seven years ago, and has had no desire to return to a "life on land" since.

Liam, on the other hand, looks nothing like a pirate. He has blond hair and fair skin and was brought up in a small town in the San Juan Islands. After graduating from the University of British Columbia, he went in search of adventure and found it working aboard a cargo ship that transported goods to Asia. After that, he spent seven years as a sailing instructor, guiding trips throughout the South Pacific and Australia on a 42-foot Whitby center cockpit. Now, he's enjoying his favorite job of all, as a crewmember on the Pacific Yellowfin.

We are definitely in good hands.

Just as we finished bringing our luggage aboard, *the* Dr. Hans Brezner descended the steps from the captain's bridge.

"Welcome aboard," he said, as he hopped off the last step to greet us.

Dr. Brezner is tall and slightly thinner than I had expected. But he certainly looks the part of a renowned scientist, with multiple pens clipped inside his breast pocket, a journal in his left hand, and a set of round spectacles resting halfway down his nose. His hair has grayed since I'd last seen a photo of him on the cover of *Earth Science* magazine a few years ago.

Captain Colin introduced everyone.

"Which of you boys is the scientist-in-training?" he asked.

"That would be my nerdy brother," Gannon said quietly to himself, but loud enough for me to hear.

I gave him a shot to the ribs with my elbow and stepped forward.

"That's me," I said, proudly.

Dr. Brezner reached out and shook my hand firmly.

"Pleasure to meet you," he said.

"It's a real honor," I said.

"So, Doctor," the captain said, "do you think you'll be able to teach this young lad a thing or two?"

The doctor replied, "I suppose I've acquired some wisdom over the years that might prove useful to a young man with an interest in the environment."

"That would be great," I said, almost at a loss for words.

"Now, if you will all follow me," the captain said, "I'll give you a quick tour of the ship."

"Yes, I have some work to do," Dr. Brezner said. "I'm sure I'll catch up with all of you later."

"I'm looking forward to it," I said.

He gave me a nod, turned, and ran back up the steps to the bridge. I still can't believe I met the great Dr. Brezner, and that he's actually on this ship with us! To me, he's a total rock star!

We followed the captain as he gave us a tour.

One hundred and fourteen feet from stem to stern and painted the color of the morning sun, the Pacific Yellowfin has quite a history. Built in 1943, this wooden ship was initially put to use as a World War II mine-setting vessel. After the war, it cruised the world, operating in many different capacities; from a floating hospital to a top-secret spy ship. Ultimately, it was purchased by Captain Colin and converted to a passenger cruiser. In recent years, the captain had restored several rooms to their original grandeur. As the captain told us prior to our arrival, "She's as much a museum as she is a boat."

The captain showed my parents to their room.

"Mom and Dad get the Owner's Stateroom," the captain said.

"Thank you, Captain," my mom said, beaming.

"Gannon and Wyatt," the captain continued, "If you'll follow me, I'll take you to the Orca Cabin down below."

The captain led us downstairs to a miniature room with a ceiling so low you'll hit your head if you stand upright. There is a writing desk in the corner. Atop the desk, is a small lamp. The room has a deep closet with shelving and space for our gear. A wooden bunk is propped against the far wall under two porthole windows.

When I put my face up to the glass, I noticed that the surface of the sea was just inches below the window. It was so close I wondered if I might see a whale swim by. I guess that's why they call it the Orca Cabin.

"Adequate accommodations?" the captain asked.

"It will do," Gannon said with a smile.

"Good. Then go ahead and get yourselves situated. We're lifting anchor in ten minutes."

"Yes, Cap'n Colin," Gannon said with a playful salute.

"I hope you brought along plenty of courage," the captain said. "I've arranged a bear-viewing excursion with Alu, an expert guide from Hartley Bay. It begins at first light, and the area you'll be exploring is prime grizzly habitat."

Gannon gulped.

"Do you really think we'll see a bear?" he asked.

"I'm almost certain of it. They don't call it the Great Bear Rainforest for nothing."

Tipping his hat, the captain turned and walked out of the room.

I could tell Gannon was nervous.

"Don't worry about it," I said. "I'm sure our bear guide will be armed."

"Yeah," Gannon agreed. "I'm sure you're right."

I sure hope I'm right.

GANNON

I was unpacking and trying really hard not to worry myself sick over this upcoming grizzly excursion when we heard the rattling of the anchor chain being hoisted. Wyatt yelled, "We're casting off" and darted from the cabin. I wanted to take video of our official cast off, so I grabbed my camera and bolted for the bow, taking the stairs two at a time and running through the dining area like I was being clocked in the 100-yard dash or something. The door to the aft cockpit was open and I jumped right through it without breaking stride and unfortunately ran right into Dr. Brezner. We both almost fell to ground and the papers he was carrying went flying all over the place. It was pretty much a disaster.

"I'm so sorry," I said. "Let me help you pick this up."

I knelt down and started scooping up some of his papers.

"Please don't touch my files," Dr. Brezner snapped.

"Okay," I replied, kind of startled by his tone of voice. "I was just trying to help."

The doctor went about collecting his papers like he was in some kind of hurry.

"Are you sure I can't give you a hand? I feel really bad that I . . ."

"Please leave me alone," he said. "I have lots of work to do. Even more now that you've made a mess of my files."

"I'm really sorry."

The doctor stood up, his papers pressed to his chest in disarray. He took a deep breath. Judging by the troubled look on his face, I thought he was about to tell me that I must be some kind of bonehead for running through the ship like that. Of course, I would have deserved it if he did, but he didn't.

"Next time please be more careful," he said, almost calmly. "No running on the ship. Understand?"

"I do," I said. "No more running. I promise."

Dr. Brezner turned and walked off.

I kind of lost the desire to video our departure or do anything for that matter, so I came back to our cabin and am watching the water pass just below the porthole window and feeling like a complete moron for what happened and at the same time wondering why Dr. Brezner was so protective of his papers. The way he acted, it was almost like he was hiding something.

WYATT

5:51 PM
GREAT BEAR RAINFOREST, 52° 37′ N   128° 53′ W
13° CELSIUS, 60° FAHRENHEIT
LIGHT DRIZZLE, WIND 10-15 MPH

Climbing several sets of steps and a couple ladders, I made my way to the top deck. The engines rumbled and came to life and the propeller churned up the water with such force, the boat seemed to lurch forward. A low-lying fog closed in behind us, and just like that, the little town of Bella Bella disappeared.

Taking in the scenery over the ship's bridge I see only wilderness ahead, vast and untamed. I can only imagine this is how Captain Vancouver must have felt when he first sailed these waters over 200 years ago, full of wonder and excitement. The real adventure has begun, and I can't wipe the smile off my face.

Our journey begins . . .

PART II

PLIGHT OF THE RAINFOREST

WYATT

SEPTEMBER 19, 6:53 AM
CARTER BAY, B.C., 52° 50' N   128° 12' W
10° CELCIUS, 51° FAHRENHEIT
DARK SKIES

After spending the night anchored in the calm waters of Carter Bay, we boarded a skiff with our bear guide, Alu, waved good-bye to Joe and Liam, and paddled toward the shore. It was just before daybreak. There was a quiet like I've never experienced. Our paddles made the loudest sound, a trickle that came with each stroke of the oar.

The early morning light kept the forest shrouded in mystery. Nearing the mouth of a narrow river, I thought I saw something move through the trees just up from the shore. But before I could point it out to my parents, it had vanished.

As we came ashore, the skiff crunched over the barnacle-crusted rocks. I stepped from the boat, planted my foot on a slippery rock, and jumped onto the beach. When I landed, my boots sunk ankle deep into the muck. I pulled myself free and walked up a hill onto the grass flats. One by one we all came ashore without incident. The last to disembark, my dad gave the skiff a shove.

The view as we paddled ashore

Drifting away from the shore, Captain Colin watched us with an eerie smirk. I had the feeling he was quietly chuckling under his breath at the thought of our faces when we encountered our first grizzly. I waved and noticed my hand was trembling every so slightly. The captain tipped his hat, grabbed the oars, and paddled away.

Not a word was spoken.

I turned and looked into the dense forest, expecting to see something staring back at me. A cold wind swept down from the mountain. Alu motioned for us to follow close behind and started toward the forest. She is a calm, contemplative girl who, according to legend, has spent many years living among the bears. Now here's the unbelievable part: She's only fifteen years old!

Though we were assured Alu is as qualified as any bear guide in the rainforest, I'd feel more comfortable if Dr. Brezner had joined us on this expedition. This morning, however, the captain explained that Dr. Brezner was so busy preparing for the expedition on Princess Royal Island that he wouldn't have time to partake in our bear viewing. I'm definitely disappointed, but at the moment I have other things to worry about—surviving the day being at the top of the list.

My heart is racing. Adrenaline is pulsing through my veins. My eyes and ears are on heightened alert. Inside this forest lurks some of the most ferocious creatures on earth. And we're on a mission to find them!

GANNON
SEPTEMBER 19
MID-MORNING

I'll be honest, there are times when I question my family's intelligence. Or should I say, lack thereof. True, I was up for this adventure in the beginning, but that's before I knew what I was getting myself into.

Bear claw markings in the mud

Now, I know.

I mean, who in their right mind marches unarmed into a cold, mud-soaked rainforest in search of giant grizzly bears? The answer to that question is no one. At least no one with any sense. Now, these people, the kind without sense, they're called crazy people. So, are we crazy? Well, if I were under oath and being questioned in a court of law, I'd have no choice but to clear my throat and say:

"Yes, your honor. We are crazy."

I should clarify what I wrote about being "unarmed." That's not completely true. We have a gun. A cap gun!

The cap gun is called a bear banger and it looks a lot like the kind of cap gun you can buy at any old toy store, but makes a slightly louder "bang" when you pull the trigger. It's supposed to scare the bear, causing it to turn and high-tail it in the other direction. But, come on. Will a cap gun really scare an 800-pound grizzly? I have serious doubts. And what if the grizzly has a hearing impairment?

It all sounded great when the captain explained bear track-ing over the phone, but now that I'm actually doing it . . . uh, not so much.

Since just after dawn, we've been seated on a slimy rock in the middle of a shallow river that stretches about a hundred feet from one side to the other. In the water, a few dozen Coho and Pink salmon thrust themselves upstream to spawn. On one side of the river there is a bear trail that leads to the water's edge and on the other side of the river, that's right, another bear trail! So, just to clarify, we're seated dead smack in the middle of two clearly worn, frequently used bear trails!

Here's the craziest part: we intentionally picked this spot because it's here that we have the greatest chance of seeing one of these mighty beasts. Last September, we were told, it was common to see several grizzly bears pass by this very rock in a single day.

And did I mention that it's cold and raining? Okay, that's not totally true. It's cold and pouring. Seriously, it's like a monsoon out here. The rain hasn't stopped coming down since we stepped ashore. Nature is leaving no question as to why they call this a rainforest.

On either side of the river, there are a handful of half-eaten salmon carcasses strewn about the rocks. Apparently, bears prefer to feast on salmon eggs, so they typically eat only the midsection of female salmon. Wolves, on the other hand, enjoy the head and brains of the salmon, so headless fish mean one thing—wolves are nearby!

Which leads me to another point. Not only are we potentially in the path of grizzlies, we might very well find ourselves surrounded by a pack of wolves! Wolves are the rainforest's apex predator, which means that this animal sits at the top of the food chain. Or, in other words, against a pack of wolves, not even the most ferocious grizzly stands a chance. No joke, scientists have actually found adult grizzly claws in wolf scat, which means that a hungry pack of wolves can and will attack, kill, and eat a full-grown grizzly bear.

Come to think of it, this experience is a lot like jumping out of a boat in the middle of the ocean with a bucket of chum and waiting for a school of great white sharks to show up for lunch.

There, I think I've made my case. It's pretty obvious we're not of sound mind, but over time we've gotten a taste for adventure and that makes you do lots of things that most people would consider insane. What can I say, it's addicting.

WYATT

SEPTEMBER 19, 11:29 AM
13° CELSIUS, 55° FAHRENHEIT
CLOUDY SKIES, WINDS 5-10 MPH

Waiting for bears to feed in the stream

Bear viewing, to be completely honest, can be pretty darn boring. At least, that's the case when there aren't any bears around. There are bugs around, that's for sure. Whenever the rain lets up, mosquitoes appear in small swarms. Dozens have made their way under the hood of my jacket. I hear them buzzing in my ear and feel them biting my cheeks. We're constantly swatting them away. Watching my parents is especially entertaining. They look like a couple of klutzy karate students practicing their chops.

The upside to all of this sitting around is that it gives us time to work on our journals. Of course, writing in a rainforest is a bit tricky. I've draped a tarp over my head, creating a small area that's protected when the rain comes so I can write without getting my pages wet. So far, it's working pretty well.

I always wondered how the great explorers like Ernest Shackleton and Sir Richard Francis Burton or Captain James Cook had the time to take such detailed notes during their epic journeys. But it's pretty obvious now. Even in the midst of the most thrilling adventures, you spend lots of time waiting. Waiting for a boat or plane, waiting for the weather to clear, or in this case, for a bear to appear. For an explorer, waiting is just part of the job.

Which leads me to the SECOND LAW OF EXPLORATION: Always maintain a healthy curiosity.

When things get boring, curiosity is what drives you forward and right now I'm as anxious as I could be to see a grizzly!

GANNON
AFTERNOON, PROBABLY

Now, aside from the fact that this excursion is crazy, I have to admit that I do appreciate being here, sitting in the cold drizzle, on this rock among all these humongous trees. This place is beautiful in any light, but when the sun comes out and sends beams of light through the forest's canopy, it's just magic—with mist rising up through the trees and raindrops sparkling like gems atop the leaves and the stream shimmering in the bright spots. Even the rocks have come alive, glistening under the sun's warm glow.

Trees covered in moss are a common sight

The forests of the Great Bear are dense and high and ancient, and I'm not using the term "ancient" loosely. This morning, the captain told us there are trees in this rainforest that are more than 1,500 years old. That means some of these trees around me were already 1,000 years old when Christopher Columbus sailed to America and that's just totally mind-blowing!

As impressive to me as the forest itself is our bear guide, Alu. When we were told that we'd have a bear guide leading us through the rainforest, I sure as heck didn't picture someone like Alu. I pictured a big, burly guy with a bushy gray beard, bad teeth, and worse breath. The bear guide I imagined wore faded overalls, a coat made of wolf fur, and had a rope of grizzly claws hanging around his neck.

When Alu walked into the galley last night with Captain Colin, I thought she was a schoolgirl from a nearby village who had come aboard for a visit. Then Captain Colin put his arm on her shoulder and said something that just about knocked me out of my chair.

"I'd like you to meet your bear guide, Alu."

My mom actually laughed out loud. She thought the captain was joking. I mean, we all did.

"I assure you," Captain Colin continued, "you're in good hands. She may be young according to the calendar, but when it comes to wisdom she's a tribal elder."

"I am from the Gitga'tt tribe and have grown up in this

forest," Alu said. "Over the years my father and mother taught me how to be one with nature so I am perfectly at ease in the Great Bear. This is my home and I promise you, I know the forest and all of its inhabitants as well as anybody."

"That's wonderful," my mom said and pulled Captain Colin into the hallway to discuss the matter in private and make sure he hadn't completely lost his mind.

My mother needed to be totally convinced that Alu knew what she was doing and I can't blame her. I mean, I wasn't thrilled about a fifteen-year-old leading us into grizzly territory either. I wanted the big, burly, bearded guy I described earlier.

As we stood around waiting for the whole thing to be sorted out, I felt like I needed to say something just to break the awkward silence.

"Nda wila waalu?" I asked Alu.

A beautiful smile came over her face.

"Aam wila waalu," she said. "Very impressive. It is not often that I can speak Gitga'tt with anyone outside my tribe. How much of our language do you know?"

"Unfortunately, that's about it. I learned it from a book I found on the boat last night."

My mom returned to the galley. Whatever Captain Colin had said completely settled her down.

"I'm sorry," she said and shook Alu's hand. "I'm Patti and

these are my sons Gannon and Wyatt. We're very excited to be here and honored to have you as our guide."

"It is a pleasure to meet you," Alu said. "When all is said and done, you will leave the Great Bear Rainforest having had a magical experience. This I promise."

Just then, my dad walked into the galley.

"Dad," Wyatt said with a smirk, "meet our bear guide, Alu."

My dad, too, laughed aloud, and we went through the whole embarrassing routine one more time.

With her light-brown complexion, dark, piercing eyes and long, flowing, black hair, Alu kind of reminds me of a young Pocahontas. She's a member of the First Nation people, which are the indigenous people of Canada. As for her name, Alu told me it means a clear night when the moon is full and illuminates its path with a golden light. On such nights, travelers are promised safe passage and people gathering food on the shore can see.

Wow, I wish my name meant something cool like that!

Anyway, I'm still amazed that my parents decided to keep Alu as our guide. I mean, the ugly, Sasquatch-looking bear guide I imagined would tie a grizzly in a knot and drop kick him into the river. He'd fight off a hungry pack of wolves with a spear he'd carved with his own hands. Alu, on the other hand, well, she's this little petite teenager without any weapons. What's she going to do if we're attacked?

I guess I just have to hope we never find out.

WYATT

More than once I could have sworn I saw something moving in the bushes, just up from the bank. Each time I get my camera ready, hold my breath, and wait. But, if there are bears nearby, they always wander deeper into the forest, away from the stream.

Before trekking into the forest, Alu explained to us what we should do if we encounter a bear. What I didn't realize is that there are different strategies for black bears, which we have at home in Colorado, versus grizzly bears.

"If we see a black bear that's grinding its teeth or shaking its head back and forth," she said, "that's a sign that it's aggravated and may become aggressive. In this case, we'll want to stand up tall, hold our arms in the air, and make lots of noise. We want to appear as big and menacing as possible. This should discourage a black bear from attacking.

"If we encounter a grizzly, crouch down and avoid making eye contact. Stay perfectly still and don't make any noise. A grizzly is not likely to back down from a challenge."

"Most important in either case is to stay calm. Bears, especially grizzlies, can sense tension. If they feel they're being threatened they'll become defensive and that's when they are likely to attack. If we appear harmless, they will know. They are very intelligent animals."

"What if a bear charges us?" my mom asked.

Alu thought for a moment, as if replaying an experience in her mind.

"Truthfully," she said, "it can be very traumatic. You would be amazed at how fast they come at you. If it happens, hold your ground. This is extremely difficult, but we're not going to outrun a bear so there is no point in trying. You have to be strong and endure it. Most likely it is a mock charge and the bear will stop."

"Bears mock charge just like lions?" I asked.

"That's right. But, if a bear actually attacks, fall to the ground, curl into a fetal position, cup your hands around the back of your neck, and play dead. In a worst-case scenario, we may need to fight it off. Should any of this happen, I will direct you. It's important that we all stay close. Our strength is in numbers."

"Well," Gannon said, "this sure sounds like tons of fun, but I think I'll stay aboard the boat and help the captain chart our course to Princess Royal Island."

"Come on, Gannon," the captain said. "Where's your sense of adventure? You didn't come all the way to the Great Bear Rainforest to sit aboard a ship. You came here to explore, to bond with nature, to view the wildlife!"

Gannon thought for a moment before he responded.

"All right," he said. "I'll go. But I'd like to state the following on record: If I become a grizzly snack, I hold Captain Colin personally responsible."

The captain gave a great, belly laugh.

"You'll be fine, laddy."

"Remember," Alu said, "we are here to observe. If we behave properly the bears won't pay any attention to us."

"I'll keep my fingers crossed," Gannon said.

My nerves have settled, replaced by a bone-numbing cold. It's not so much the temperature. It's well above freezing right now. It's all this rain. My hands are shaking and my writing is starting to look more like a seismographic chart than anything else. What I wouldn't do to warm myself by a nice campfire right about now!

GANNON

After what seemed like forever without a sighting, Alu leaned to me and whispered.

"I am concerned that we have not seen a bear today," she said.

Concerned isn't the word I'd use. My feelings over the matter are a combination of disappointment and relief, really. A contradiction, I know, but true. I mean, of course, I'd love to see a grizzly in the wild. I have my video camera all wrapped up in a waterproof casing and have been thinking about how great it would be to get footage of one stepping from the woods, lumbering toward the river, stopping, and looking me in the eyes. Oh, man, to capture that on video would just be awesome! Besides, we are here to see bears, so bears we must see. At the same time, I sure as heck don't want to be mauled by one!

"Notice the salmon swimming upstream," Alu continued, speaking so softly I could barely hear her over the trickle of the stream. "This is only a fraction of the salmon that we typically see here. Last year, numbers were down considerably. This year it is even worse. I don't understand. The stream should be so full of salmon that you can't even see the bottom."

How the salmon numbers could fall off so drastically, I have no idea. And I didn't ask either because Alu seemed to be lost in her own thoughts and, well, I didn't want to bother her. I mean, she's a real quiet, introspective type person, in general, but the troubled look in her eyes tells me that something in the Great Bear Rainforest is terribly wrong.

WYATT
2:28 PM

We were all getting a little restless when Alu spoke to us in a whisper: "We'll stay put for a little while longer, then I'd like to hike up the mountain a few kilometers to check on a grizzly den that I know of. I completely understand if some of you are not comfortable joining me. I'd be happy to take you back to the shoreline where we can radio the captain to pick you up."

Even though we haven't seen any wildlife, I'm happy with my field notes and the photos I've taken today, and besides, there will be more opportunities to view bears when we get to Princess Royal Island. I'm also eager to talk more with Dr. Brezner, so, without question, I'm ready for the warmth and safety of the Pacific Yellowfin.

I figured I wouldn't be the only one. Given the fact that he's been nervous about this whole bear viewing business from the start, I was sure Gannon would vote to double time it back to the ship. But just when you think you've got Gannon pegged, he'll completely blindside you.

"I'll go," he said.

"Where?" I asked. "Back to the ship? Sounds good. I'll go with you."

"No, not to the ship," Gannon said. "To the bear den."

I could've killed him.

"Do you think there will be cubs inside?" he asked.

"We'll have to see," Alu said, somberly.

"Wyatt," my mom whispered, "you in?"

"Of course I'm in."

What else could I say?

"Then it's agreed," my dad said. "We'll all go to the den together. A good, uphill hike will get the blood flowing and warm us up. It's just what we need."

So, the journey continues . . .

GANNON

The rugged, mountainous interior of the GBR

Hiking into the mountains in this sopping wet place is beyond grueling. My socks are completely soaked and squishing around inside my rubber rain boots, and these boots don't have the best traction, and even worse support, and the slopes we're moving up are steep and slick, making it even more difficult to get any kind of footing. At times we've had to pull each other up muddy embankments and squeeze under fallen trees and sidestep around massive boulders.

Funny thing happened, though. I tripped, which isn't the funny part, of course. The funny part is that as I was going down I reached out for Wyatt to break my fall and accidently yanked his pants down around his ankles. Oh, man, he got so mad and almost fell over himself trying to pull his pants back up before anyone saw.

"Purple polka dots, Wyatt? Really?"

"Mom bought them for me. You probably have a pair, too," he said and stormed off.

"Whatever!" I yelled.

He hasn't talked to me since.

We're about an hour into this slog and have stopped for a rest and thank goodness for that because if we hadn't, I'd have probably fallen flat on my face and stayed there for good.

WYATT
4:07 PM
1,978 FEET ABOVE SEA LEVEL (603 METERS)
10° CELSIUS, 50° FAHRENHEIT
CLOUDY, WIND 10-20 MPH

As we came to a clearing in the woods, Alu held out her hand, signaling for us to stay back. Just ahead was a cluster of large granite boulders. At the base of the rocks was a dark opening. This was the den. Inside, possibly, were grizzly bears.

My hair stood on end as Alu stepped quietly toward the den. Approaching a dark opening in the rocks where a giant grizzly might jump out and tear you apart didn't seem like a smart move, but I envied Alu's bravery.

She stood at the entrance, placed her hand on the rock

and slowly leaned inside to take a look. Again, my heart was racing. Then, without warning, she disappeared into the darkness.

I looked back at Gannon and my parents. Their eyes were as wide as saucers. I'm sure we were all wondering the same thing: "Are we about to witness a grizzly attack?"

She was probably inside no more than sixty seconds, but it seemed like hours. I moved closer to the rocks and listened for sounds coming from inside the den. I almost expected to hear a cry for help.

When Alu emerged from the den, she appeared deep in thought. She took a moment before she said anything, staring off into the distance, as if quietly trying to solve a riddle.

Finally, she spoke.

"Unfortunately, this family did not make it through the winter," she said, her voice grim.

"What do you mean?" Gannon asked.

"A mother and two cubs," she said, "they died."

"How?" Gannon asked.

"Starvation."

"How could that happen?" I asked.

"Salmon are the primary food source for many species including bears," Alu continued. "But the salmon numbers were so low last year they weren't able to eat enough to make it through the winter. There are even fewer salmon this year. I'm afraid more bears and many other animals that depend on the salmon for food may die, as well."

"Can we see them?" Gannon asked.

"Of course," Alu said. "Follow me."

Alu led us into the dark, damp confines of the den. There was a terrible stench inside that made it difficult to breathe. I pulled my jacket up over my nose, which helped a little. At first, it was impossible to see anything. We all just stood there, waiting for our eyes to adjust to the darkness, knowing that a family of grizzlies lay at our feet. In time, I could make out the large, arching back of the mother. At its highest point, her back measured to my waist—and she was lying down. This was a massive grizzly! Probably close to eight-feet tall if she stood on her hind legs. I couldn't imagine that this creature, so peaceful looking there in the den, had ever possessed the ferociousness that I'd read so much about.

The cubs were tiny clones of their mother. They had already lost much of their fur and their hipbones and ribs were visible through their pale skin. Otherwise, it looked as if they were still hibernating. Enjoying a prolonged sleep while they waited for the warmth of spring.

I keep wondering why the salmon numbers have declined so significantly over the past two years. Could it be that the offshore fishermen are catching too many of them? Over-fishing has decimated fish populations in other areas of the world. Is it now happening in British Columbia?

I'm anxious to talk to Dr. Brezner when we return to the ship. I'm sure that he'll have an explanation.

GANNON
DINNERTIME
MOOD: IMPROVING

A sight for sore eyes . . . the Pacific Yellowfin

I can't put into words how good it feels to be back aboard the Pacific Yellowfin. This day has been exhausting, to say the least, and I've been really upset since we found those poor grizzlies in their den, but there is something about Captain Colin and his ship that make me feel like everything is going to be all right.

After cleaning up, we all gathered in the galley where Joe served us a pot of seafood stew that smelled so good it made my mouth water. Steam rose from the soup as he poured it into our bowls. It was full of shrimp and scallops and mussels, all of it swimming in a spicy red sauce. After a day eating nothing but trail mix and beef jerky, I was so hungry the sole of a shoe would have tasted good. So, needless to say, the stew did not disappoint.

To cheer us up even more, Captain Colin came strolling into the galley after dinner with a guitar under his arm.

"Does anyone mind if I strum a few tunes?" he asked.

"We'd love it," my mom said.

"Great. Everyone feel free to sing along."

Now, I'm no concert vocalist by any stretch, but I definitely enjoy belting out a tune every now and again. My favorite from the captain's playlist was, "The Whistling Gypsy," which I sang with gusto:

> "Gypsy rover, come over the hill,
> down through the valley so shady.
> He whistled and he sang til the green woods rang
> and he won the heart of a lady!"

My parents got up and danced around the galley and Alu tapped out a drumbeat atop the table. Wyatt even joined in, singing off-key backup vocals when he knew the words, and even when he didn't.

After the sing-along, we said good-bye to Alu and she told us that we would see her again in a couple days on Princess Royal Island, where we would spend time searching for the spirit bear. I mean, after all we've been through today, setting off into the woods to look for bears again should be the last thing I want to do, but I can't help but get excited by the possibility of seeing this rare and magnificent animal.

WYATT
11:02 PM

After Liam and Alu boarded the tender and drove into the darkness toward Alu's home in Hartley Bay, I saw Dr. Brezner walking across the aft cockpit.

"Hello, Dr. Brezner," I said timidly as I approached.

"Hi there, Wyatt," he said. "How was your bear viewing excursion?"

"Well, about that," I said, "I was wondering if I could ask you a couple quick questions."

Dr. Brezner took a glance at his watch.

"Okay," he said, "I have a few minutes."

"I don't know if you heard, but we found a mother grizzly and two cubs dead in their den."

"No, I've been working in my cabin all day and didn't hear anything about it," he said. "I'm sorry."

"Alu believes they starved to death because there weren't enough salmon to eat. Even today, there were very few in the stream. Alu said there are usually thousands. I was wondering if you knew what might cause such a drastic decline in the salmon population."

Dr. Brezner gave me an inquisitive look, as if he had been caught off guard.

"Do you have any scientific data supporting your claim that the salmon population has declined?"

"Well, no. It was just an observation Alu made today."

"Wyatt," he said, "Alu is not a scientist. An observation is only a starting point that may lead one to conduct further research. By no means should a single observation be used to conclude that something is fact."

True, Doctor Brezner was correct in some ways. There are rules to follow and many steps involved in determining that something is scientific fact. However, anyone with a curiosity for the environment must consider the beliefs and intuition of the native people. Members of the First Nation do not need to form a hypothesis or collect thousands of pages of scientific data to support their beliefs. They have 10,000 years of history in the area. Their knowledge comes from experience and is passed down from generation to generation. When they feel something is wrong, it usually is.

"I understand," I said, "but Alu has lived in the forest her whole life. She knows this ecosystem as well as anyone. Something isn't right. She said the salmon numbers were down last year, too. There could be a new disease that's reducing the population or maybe something has changed in the water, or maybe it's the result of overfishing. There has to be a reason why so many of the salmon are not making it back to spawn. You know as well as I that salmon are a keystone species. The bears and many other species depend on them for their survival. I thought maybe you could look into it while you're doing research on Princess Royal Island."

Dr. Brezner placed his hand on my shoulder.

"Let me explain something to you, Wyatt," he said calmly. "Change is part of nature. Just because someone observes a recurring event over several years, or decades even, doesn't mean that this event will continue indefinitely into the future. Things are always changing. Glaciers advance and retreat. Species go extinct. Others adapt. This is part of the earth's natural evolution, and it applies to all things."

"Then you're not concerned about the salmon?" I asked.

"Again, you're speaking of one stream out of hundreds that flow through these coastal mountains. Until you've studied a larger sample, and done so thoroughly, you have no way of knowing whether or not there is a problem."

Based on Alu's concern, I had been certain that there was a problem, a problem that needed to be brought to the doctor's attention. But after speaking with him, I feel foolish having even brought it up.

He could tell I was embarrassed and patted me on the back.

"You know, Wyatt," he said, "you remind me a lot of myself when I was your age."

"I do?"

"Absolutely. You're curious about the environment and how it works, just like I was. You have a love of nature and are concerned by the things you feel may be a threat."

I nodded my head, soaking up his praise.

"At your age, I was concerned, too." He chuckled. "I still am, of course. But you must understand, nature is resilient. Despite all we humans do to disrupt the environment, nature has the ability to sort things out. It is more powerful than us. In the end, nature will always prevail."

These statements seemed to contradict a life's work protecting nature, but even so, hearing this explanation from a scientist of his stature did comfort me. Not that I've totally dismissed Alu's belief that something is amiss, but if Dr. Brezner feels the decline in salmon is nothing to be concerned about, that nature will ultimately take care of itself, who am I to argue?

"Thanks for your insight, Dr. Brezner," I said. "I really appreciate your time."

"My pleasure," he said. "It's inspiring to see a young man with your passion. You are inquisitive and bright. Keep it up and you will accomplish great things."

It's much later now as I sit and write by lamplight in my cabin, but after that compliment from Dr. Brezner, falling asleep would be impossible. I'm on top of the world! I don't know what to do with myself. Maybe I'll reread his essay on environmental toxicology and then try to catch some shut-eye.

More tomorrow . . .

GANNON

It seemed I had just fallen asleep when Captain Colin woke me up.

"All hands on deck!" he hollered from the galley. "Breakfast is served!"

"I'm not hungry!" I shouted back, pulling the covers up over my head.

"Hungry or not, I need you up here on the double!"

Still in my clothes from the night before, I rolled out of bed and climbed the ladder to the galley. They had put out a big spread of hot food for us and I filled my plate with scrambled eggs and bacon and potatoes and a few slices of buttered toast. The smell of fresh coffee was in the air and I'm no coffee drinker, but this morning I thought seriously about becoming one.

"In a few hours, I'm going ashore with Dr. Brezner," the captain said. "While I'm gone, I'll need you and Wyatt to assist Liam with a few tasks."

"Oh, goodie," I said.

"We'd be happy to," Wyatt said.

Boy, Wyatt can be a real butt kisser sometimes.

"The bow could use a good scrubbing," he said. "The galley, as well. Liam will show you where we keep the mops."

"What does this have to do with finding a spirit bear?" I asked.

"Every sailor aboard my ship must earn his keep. Besides, chores are an important part of a young man's upbringing. They help build character."

"Oh, jeez. You sound just like my parents," I said.

Liam had an ear-to-ear grin, and why wouldn't he? Looks like we'll be doing his dirty work. Normally, I'd be frustrated to no end. I think I've made it pretty clear just how much I dislike chores, but even though I hate to admit it, the captain is right. We need to earn our keep. After all, this isn't some kind of a leisure cruise where you loaf around all day drinking fruity drinks with umbrellas in them. We're in the midst of a great exploration! And during any exploration you have to do whatever is necessary to make sure that your mission is successful. Even if it means tending to chores.

Argh, chores! I can't seem to escape them!

WYATT
SEPTEMBER 20, 11:24 AM
BETWEEN PRINCESS ROYAL AND GRIBBELL ISLANDS
53° 18' N 128° 59' W
15° CELSIUS, 59° FAHRENHEIT
CLOUDY SKIES, SLIGHT WIND

Mid-morning, we dropped anchor approximately one-half mile off the north coast of Princess Royal Island, and

Captain Colin and Dr. Brezner prepared to go ashore. I watched as several pieces of scientific equipment were packed for the journey. Included were two computers, a GPS system, radios, an antenna, journals, and a couple other devices I could not identify. Dr. Brezner appeared to be in a hurry, quickly packing his equipment into hard-shell, waterproof cases.

"Good luck with your research, Doctor," I said. "I hope you find a spirit bear."

"Yes," he said, looking up to me as he continued to pack. "A spirit bear. I'm sure we will. Thank you."

I had a hundred questions to ask him, but decided it was best that I wait until he returned from the day's expedition.

The captain took a radio and a survival pack with a first-aid kit, matches, a Swiss Army knife and a flare gun for signaling the ship in the event of an emergency. (I take inventory of these sorts of things. It's the best way to learn).

"We must be going," Dr. Brezner said to the captain, impatiently. "Time is of the essence."

With the tender loaded, the captain started the engine, filling the air with the scent of gasoline. Tipping his hat to Joe and Liam, he put the motor in reverse and backed the tender away from the ship.

"Gannon and Wyatt," he yelled, "when I get back I want the ship looking as good as the day she first came out of the boatyard!"

"Aye-aye, Captain," I said, enthusiastically.

As the captain steered the tender toward the island, I noticed for the first time a storm building over the ocean. The sky had no distinct clouds, just shades of gray, soft overhead and becoming darker and darker to the point that it was almost black on the western horizon.

"There's a big storm coming in, Captain," I yelled, as if he hadn't noticed himself.

"We're in a rainforest!" he hollered back with a smile. "There's always a storm coming in!"

"Yeah, but this one looks pretty nasty!" Gannon yelled.

"There isn't a captain on the seven seas who knows the waters and weather patterns of the Great Bear better than yours truly! I could navigate this island with my eyes closed! Don't you worry about us! We'll be just fine!"

I leaned on the cold railings and watched as the boat trolled through the rolling waters toward the mountainous, fog-shrouded wilds of Princess Royal Island.

"Heads up!" Liam yelled.

I turned just in time to catch the mop he had thrown at me.

"You may as well get started," he said. "We've got lots of work to do."

"Aye-aye," I said, this time with far less enthusiasm.

GANNON

Okay, chores are bad, regardless, but here's something I just realized, there are levels of bad—let's say 1 to 10, with 10 being the worst chores of all. Now, chores aboard a ship that's rocking back and forth in rough seas are a flat out 11. If I don't get my sea legs soon that big, hearty breakfast I ate this morning may get tossed overboard, if you know what I mean.

WYATT
2:01 PM

I had been mopping for what seemed like days when Gannon yelled from across the bow.

"Whale off the port side!"

I dropped my mop and ran to the edge of the ship, looking out over the water. I didn't see anything.

"You sure it was a whale?" I asked.

"Well, it was either a whale or a seal the size of a school bus," Gannon said.

Suddenly, thousands of bubbles floated to the surface. There were definitely whales below us. I ran inside and grabbed my camera. As soon as I returned, an enormous humpback surfaced for air only feet from the ship. It was grayish-black, with a small dorsal fin. Before its blowhole dropped below the water, it blew a mist as foul as anything I've ever smelled. If you can imagine rotten fish wrapped in dirty gym socks and stuffed in a locker for a couple years, whale mist is slightly worse.

"Oh, that's disgusting," Gannon said, covering his nose with his hand.

The tail of a humpback whale

There were four or five humpbacks swimming together. I snapped several photos, as these 40-ton mammals came up for a breath time and again. When their slimy backs broke the surface, they looked like giant serpents slithering through the water. Soon after the dorsal fins rolled back underwater, their tails came up. The undersides of their tails were white and crusted with barnacles. A waterfall would cascade from the tail and then they were gone, a bubbling pocket of water the only evidence they had been there.

"The storm is coming in fast," Liam suddenly yelled from the bridge, pointing west. "You can finish cleaning the bow later. There's plenty of work to be done inside. Come on in and take a break. I'll meet you in the galley shortly."

Looking through the circular galley windows, all I can see are dark clouds. Princess Royal Island itself is completely socked in. On a ship as big as the Pacific Yellowfin, you only feel the motion of the sea when it's really rough, and it's rough. I can't help but wonder how Captain Colin and Dr. Brezner are faring in these conditions.

GANNON
AFTERNOON OF THE 20TH

Okay, there's something strange going on and I need to stop everything for a second and get this down in my journal while it's all still fresh in my head.

Not long after we ducked inside to escape the storm, Liam hit us with our next set of chores. Wyatt was to mop the kitchen and I was to clean the guest quarters. This was all to be done before the captain returned, Liam's orders.

"Jeez," I said quietly to Wyatt, "if I'd known we were going to have to work this hard to visit the Great Bear, I might have declined Captain Colin's offer."

"Oh, come on, Gannon," Wyatt said. "If we get a chance to see a spirit bear, it will all be totally worth it."

"Yeah, I guess you're right."

"Now, get going," Wyatt said. "They'll be back soon."

I was going to start with my parents' room, but my dad was in there working on some sketches and my mom was lying on the bed reading a novel and they said they were comfortable right where they were and weren't moving, so I told them that's just fine by me, they could clean the room themselves.

Next, I moved to Dr. Brezner's cabin.

When I walked in, it reminded me of Wyatt's room, annoyingly perfect, with all his clothes neatly folded and his shoes arranged in the closet and his books and paperwork all organized and stacked on the desk, but the nice thing about cleaning up after a neat-freak is that there's really nothing to clean up. His bed wasn't completely made, that was about it, so I thought I'd straighten it up and be on my way, but that's when I came upon something interesting. It was a total accident, I swear. I wasn't snooping or anything; it just so happened that my hand brushed against something under the mattress, so, naturally, I slid it out from under the bed. It was a stack of files that looked just like the ones I knocked out of his hands. The ones he'd been so protective of.

I checked the hallway to make sure no one was coming and spread the files out on the desk. There were several maps and salmon spawning routes and grids with numbers and formulas that I couldn't understand and a report with the title:

The report was organized into sections and each section had a title like, "Analysis of Salmon Populations," and there was another one I remember called, "Economic Prospects of Timber," which was from Halliman Timber, and then there was one titled, "Pipeline Proposal," which I opened up.

Okay, at this point I'll admit, I did kind of feel like I was snooping, but this stuff was way too suspicious to ignore, so I read a couple pages about Pacific Oil's proposal to build a pipeline that runs from Alberta, far to the east, all the way to the western coast of Canada by way of the Great Bear Rainforest. Here on the coast, all the oil would be loaded into supertankers and shipped all over the world.

The thought of supertankers in these parts brings to mind all those catastrophic oil spills that have happened around the world and for that reason alone the plan seems off-the-charts nuts to me. I mean, why would anyone want to risk ruining this one-of-a-kind place?

Before I put the files away, I noticed a letter written to Dr. Brezner that was typed and unsigned. Looking over the letter as quickly as I could, I read the following:

"PER AGREED UPON TERMS, FOUR EQUAL PAYMENTS WILL BE WIRED TO SPECIFIED INTERNATIONAL ACCOUNT UPON COMPLETION OF EACH PHASE ..."

Before I could finish reading the letter, I heard footsteps

overhead and hurried to put all the files back where I'd found them. I straightened the bed sheets and moved on to the next room, wondering what the doctor was really up to. I just can't ignore my gut, and my gut tells me something fishy is going on.

Anyway, I cleaned the rest of the rooms as fast as I could and ran to look for Wyatt and ask him his thoughts on what I'd found. He was rinsing his mop on the deck.

"Wyatt," I whispered, "Would Dr. Brezner have any need for reports from oil, timber, and fishing companies?"

"I don't know," he said. "Why?"

"I found some files under his bed."

"Please tell me you weren't snooping!" Wyatt shouted.

"No, I wasn't," I said. "Honest."

"I can't believe you, Gannon! You know you shouldn't go through someone's personal things!"

"I came across the files when I was cleaning, all right? Get over it and listen to me for a second! He has timber estimates, oil pipeline drawings, information on the area's natural resources, maps showing salmon routes around Princess Royal Island, and all kinds of other stuff."

"I'm sure there's a logical explanation," Wyatt argued. "Maybe he's trying to disprove something that's in the reports so that he can protect the Great Bear Rainforest."

"The rainforest is already protected though."

"But it's a constant battle to keep it that way. The resources in the forest are worth a fortune."

"Which brings me to the most suspicious thing of all. There's a letter in his files that mentions wiring money to an international bank account."

"Dr. Brezner gets paid for his research, Gannon. That's how he makes a living. What's so suspicious about that?"

"Go take a look at the letter for yourself."

"I don't think so."

"The letter is unsigned. There's no information that could be used to trace it back to anyone. It was obviously written by a person who wants to remain anonymous. I'm telling you. Dr. Brezner is up to something."

"And I'm telling you, the doctor's intentions are honorable. He's spent his life protecting the environment. He's one of the good guys, Gannon!"

Liam came onto the bow with a worried look on his face.

"Just drop it," Wyatt said. "Here comes Liam."

"Fine," I said. "To be continued."

"We're all done, Liam!" Wyatt yelled into the wind.

Liam didn't say anything. He was staring into the fog, a radio in his hand.

"Liam!" I said, "Is everything all right?"

Liam put the radio to his mouth.

"Pacific Yellowfin to Captain Colin. Captain Colin, do you copy?"

There was no response.

"What's going on?" I asked.

Liam paused and took a deep breath before speaking: "I've lost radio contact with the captain."

WYATT

10:53 PM

Minutes have turned to hours and we still haven't heard from the captain. Naturally, everyone is afraid. The front that blew through brought some high winds and heavy rains, but it wasn't anything the captain hasn't seen a hundred times. Liam is confident they took shelter on the island and waited out the storm.

That may be the case, though it still leaves certain questions unanswered. If they did wait out the storm, which passed through several hours ago, why haven't they returned to the ship by now? It also doesn't explain why we haven't heard from them on the radio.

I hate to be pessimistic, but the outlook is not good.

We gathered in the galley with Liam, Joe, and my parents to discuss our options. Liam made it clear that as long as it was dark, the efforts of a search party would be futile. According to the weather report, another line of squalls is moving in from the northwest. These storms would make nighttime navigation difficult and extremely dangerous.

Bottom line, there is nothing we can do until daybreak. We've agreed that my parents will take the second tender and search the shoreline at first light.

I keep analyzing the situation, running it over and over in my mind. The fact that they have not communicated at all with the ship is strange. They left with two radios. That both radios would become inoperable is unlikely, but I guess not completely impossible. It's also possible that the tender was damaged in the storm while they were on shore. Still, each of the tenders has a flare gun. I am sure we would have seen one streaking through the sky if they were in trouble.

With each passing minute I am more convinced that Captain Colin and Dr. Brezner are in grave danger. I wish there was something I could do. But anchored off the coast of a dark, foreboding rainforest, I am powerless to do anything more than wait and hope for the best.

GANNON
SEPTEMBER 21
EARLY MORNING

All through the night I kept listening for the sound of a boat motor and I couldn't fall asleep and just sat there in my bed hoping that the captain would come pulling up to the ship at any moment with some incredible tale of adventure. Unfortunately, that didn't happen.

Everyone was awake and nervous and packing up the tender before the sun even came up. This is a search and rescue mission, nothing less. My parents took two radios and several days worth of food and water and a waterproof bag with sleeping bags, tarps, and all kinds of other survival gear. They aren't planning to be out overnight, but neither was the captain.

As my dad revved up the motor and backed away we tested the radios.

"Wyatt to Radio One . . . do you copy?"

"I copy," my mom said.

"Radio Two, do you copy?"

"Loud and clear," my dad said. "We'll keep regular contact. You boys help Joe and Liam take care of the ship. When we bring the captain back, you know he's going to inspect it with a fine-toothed comb."

"We've got it under control," I said. "Please be safe out there."

"You know we will."

My mom blew us a kiss as my dad turned the boat and started slowly toward the island over choppy waters and the whole time I just stood there on the bow watching until they'd disappeared into the thick fog. Soon after, the sound of the boat motor trailed off and fell silent. Since then I've been a total wreck, just sitting here in the galley bouncing my leg and biting my nails and waiting to hear something.

WYATT
SEPTEMBER 21, 9:12 AM

Overrun by nervous energy, I walked the ship, desperate for

some positive news. Each time I passed the bridge I'd holler up to Liam: "Any word?" The answer was always the same. "Nothing yet!"

I have to be honest, Gannon's discovery of what he felt were "suspicious" files in Dr. Brezner's room is troubling and my curiosity is getting the best of me. With my parents away, Joe occupied in the kitchen, and Liam stationed on the bridge, I considered slipping into Dr. Brezner's cabin to have a look. I even made my way to his room, but stopped just short of entering. It would be wrong. I know it. In fact, I just yelled at Gannon for doing what I'm anxious to do myself—snoop!

The thing is, I'm desperate to prove Gannon wrong. But to debunk his accusations, I need proof that Dr. Brezner's intentions are ethical. For that reason, maybe I could forgive myself for violating the doctor's privacy. Maybe I should take a look.

I'm torn.

Don't know what to do.

Wait, Gannon's yelling to me from above. Maybe there's news . . .

GANNON

My parents have trolled the shoreline and what they found is not good.

"Are you sure the debris is part of the captain's tender?" Joe said into the radio.

"Yes," my dad said. "We're sure. We've found a large section of the aluminum hull floating offshore. It looks like the boat was smashed to pieces in the rocks. And there's more."

My dad was quiet for a minute before continuing. Liam paced the bow. I held my breath.

"We also found the captain's hat."

Joe closed his eyes and Liam ran his fingers through his hair.

"Okay," Joe said, after regaining his composure, "but it's possible that they swam ashore. Wouldn't you agree?"

"It's definitely possible," my dad said. "We're going ashore to search the coastline. Hopefully, we'll find them safe and sound."

"We'll stand by for more news," Joe said.

"Okay," my dad said. "We'll keep you updated. Over and out."

That's the last I've heard of my father's voice.

About a half an hour has gone by and Joe's tried several times to reach my parents on the radio, but there's been no response. Nothing at all. Just silence on the other end. Again, I feel sick to my stomach. This time I might seriously throw up. My brain is being bombarded by all sorts of terrible thoughts and I'm totally panicked, about to flip out, really. I mean, my mom and dad have to be okay. They can't be dead. They just can't!

WYATT
4:47 PM

Joe and I found Gannon outside.

"We have to find them," Gannon said, his voice cracking with despair. "We need to get to the island right away."

"So you can disappear, too?" Joe said. "I won't allow it. It's far too dangerous. Very few people have ventured into the interior of Princess Royal Island. And some that have were never seen again. It will be dark in four hours. Even in the daylight hours the forest can be so dense you can't see the sunlight through the trees. It's easy to lose all sense of direction. You can literally be a hundred meters from the shoreline and be completely lost."

"But we can't just leave them out there," Gannon continued. "They need our help. They could be hurt. We might be the only ones who can save their lives!"

"I'm calling the Coast Guard. I should have called them right after we lost radio contact with Captain Colin and Dr. Brezner, but I was confident they would be okay. To me, the captain's always been invincible."

"It's not your fault," I said. "We all thought they'd be okay."

WYATT

Another hour has passed and I don't think we have a choice anymore. We have to take action. To be honest, I'm scared. But, there are lots of reasons for Gannon and I to go in search of the captain, Dr. Brezner, and my parents—all of them good. The best of which is that right now we are their only hope.

Turns out, the Coast Guard is responding to another Mayday call. A cargo ship is taking on water off the western coast of Haida Gwaii, a group of islands more than one hundred miles away, and that mission is putting to use the only rescue boat and helicopter in the region. Right now, we're in one of the most remote parts of the Great Bear Rainforest, almost a day's travel from civilization. Even in the best circumstances, it can take a long time before help gets to you.

As further motivation to go ashore, Gannon reminded me that, according to seafaring folklore, a ship whose captain has been lost at sea becomes a "ghost ship." Legend has it that a ghost ship is doomed to float adrift at sea . . . forever! Now, I try not to be superstitious. Gannon, on the other hand, can't help himself and sometimes he can be pretty convincing.

"Did you hear that, Wyatt?" he asked.

"What?" I asked.

"I just heard the captain's voice."

We ran to the starboard side of the ship. Then the port side. There was no sign of the captain. No boat. No anything.

"You're losing it," I said.

"No, I'm not!" Gannon yelled. "I'm telling you, I heard the captain!"

Gannon paused, as if thinking.

"Oh, man," he said, "I just remembered something."

"What?"

"This was a hospital ship at one time. Jeez, you know how many ghosts are probably floating around us right now? I can literally feel them breathing down my neck!"

Gannon shuddered, spun around, and hightailed it through the galley. I followed him to our room, where he haphazardly went about packing a waterproof bag with supplies.

"What are you doing?" I asked.

"I'll never forgive myself if we don't do everything we can to save Mom and Dad," he said. "Plus, there's no way I'm staying aboard this ghost ship any longer than I have to."

"Do you understand how dangerous it would be to travel to that island alone?"

"I don't know about you, but I learned a lot about the rainforest from Alu yesterday. I'm confident I'll be okay."

I folded my arms and paced the room.

"Let's just take a minute to think this through," I said.

"I don't need a minute. My mind is made up. The way

I see it, you have a choice. You can either come with me or enjoy a night aboard a haunted ship."

"You know Joe and Liam aren't going to let you go anywhere."

"They aren't going to know. The next time they go down to the engine room, I'm going to sneak off the ship."

"And just how do you plan to sneak off the ship? Both tenders are gone and you can't unload the skiff without Joe's help."

"I'll take one of the kayaks. I'll be on the island before they know I'm gone."

Gannon wasn't giving me much of a choice. He was going ashore no matter what.

"Okay, fine," I said. "Give me ten minutes to pack. I'm coming with you."

As the THIRD LAW OF EXPLORATION states: Make certain you are properly equipped before embarking on an adventure.

The difference between a properly equipped explorer and a poorly equipped explorer can be life or death. It's that simple.

Much like preparing for travel, packing for a search and rescue mission isn't something you want to do in a hurry. But again, I had no choice. Time was short. I grabbed another waterproof backpack and quickly went to work.

After packing, I pulled the latest weather report from the bridge and read that there's another front coming off the

Pacific Ocean. We can't catch a break. These storm fronts keep coming at us, one right after another. And this one is bringing colder temperatures.

In the captain's library, I found a topographical map of Princess Royal Island and some general information about the area to take with us.

We have to be careful not to raise the suspicions of Joe or Liam. If they catch us preparing for this mission, we won't be going anywhere.

GANNON
A FEW HOURS BEFORE DUSK
FEAR FACTOR: HIGH

Princess Royal Island rising above the clouds

Okay, Wyatt and I are all set. Our packs are under a tarp and the kayaks are near the edge of the boat for an easy drop. Our fingers are crossed that Liam and Joe won't notice. Now, all we have to do is wait for them to disappear into the bowels of the ship. As soon as they do, we launch for Princess Royal Island!

GANNON
10:02 PM

About two hours before sundown, Liam and Joe finally disappeared into the engine room and Wyatt and I went to work sliding the kayaks over the side of the ship and carefully climbing aboard. A pretty strong wind blew over the water making the surface really choppy with white-caps breaking over the front of the kayaks and knocking us around and we had to work hard to keep from getting dumped into the Pacific.

Within minutes of leaving the Pacific Yellowfin, we were totally surrounded by fog and what we had been able to see of the island disappeared. In that fog, it felt like we were all alone, paddling in the middle of the ocean, but we knew that if we continued moving west we'd eventually run right into the island, so that's what we did.

Getting to Princess Royal took a lot longer than we thought, mostly because a strong headwind and rough condi-tions made for slow going. There were times where it seemed like we weren't making any progress at all, or were even going backward, but eventually we broke through the fog and the rocky shoreline came into view.

As we got closer to the coastline, I spotted a lone wolf staring at us from atop a boulder field that spilled onto the beach. I turned back to Wyatt, pointing to the wolf, and we both stopped paddling and sat patiently in the gently rolling waves, hoping that he would eventually move along.

The wolf was thin, a trait Alu had said is common among the coastal species, but his scrawny figure didn't make him any less menacing, that's for sure. His gaze alone sent this wave of fear right through me. As intimidating as they are, wolves really are beautiful animals. This one had a mostly gray coat with some streaks of black on its belly. I couldn't tell for sure, but it almost looked like the area around its mouth was covered in blood and that kind of freaked me out.

For a while the wolf didn't move. He just sort of stood there, staring, like he was guarding his territory or something. Wyatt and I kept drifting closer, carried by the current. The wolf didn't seem to appreciate the fact that we were invading his personal space and eventually gave a great howl that sounded like it came from the depths of his lungs. I paddled backward a few strokes and was seriously thinking about going back to the ship, when the wolf turned and trotted off into the woods.

We didn't know if the wolf was rounding up his buddies or hiding in the trees, ready to attack when we came ashore, so we paddled in the opposite direction to put a safe distance between ourselves and this top-of-the-food-chain predator. A little ways north we found a tributary and just beyond that a beachhead of small boulders and it was there that we came ashore.

Along the shoreline we found a few fresh salmon carcasses scattered about the barnacled rocks.

"Notice that the heads are all missing," Wyatt said, pointing at the salmon carcasses. "That means that they were eaten by wolves."

"Thank you, Captain Obvious," I said.

Wyatt rolled his eyes.

A salmon carcass left by a wolf

It seems that there's really no way to avoid wolves on this island, so we continued ashore. Getting ourselves onto the island was tricky with the slimy, algae-coated rocks making it almost impossible to get any traction, especially when dragging a heavy kayak. Wyatt took a hard fall, rolling backward into a shallow pool and was soaking wet and cold, but fortunately he wasn't hurt, well, except for his pride.

Not sure how high the water would reach when the tide came in, we've dragged our kayaks up a hill a good distance and stashed them inside the forest.

"We need to set up camp right away," Wyatt said. "We probably have a half an hour of light left, at best. Let's go further up this hill, underneath those trees. You put up the tarp, and I'll get a fire going. I'm going to freeze if I don't dry out these clothes. And maybe Mom and Dad will see the smoke."

I took the tarps and a line of rope and Wyatt went around gathering whatever dry wood he could find. I walked into the forest and looked for a soft bed of moss with a good canopy of trees overhead to keep the rain off. The light was almost gone from the sky by the time I found a decent campsite—a patch of flat ground between two fallen spruce trees, about seven feet by ten maybe, with good tree coverage.

I was in a race with the dark and strung the triangular tarp between two trees and staked the third corner of the tarp to the ground, driving the stake deep into the soil with a rock. With the tarps in place, I cleared the rocks and fallen tree branches underneath and padded the ground with extra moss and then placed the second tarp over the moss and spread out our sleeping bags. The last thing I did was to string our food over a high tree limb, beyond the reach of bears and wolves.

I figured Joe and Liam had noticed we were gone, so I called them on the radio to let them know we were okay, but all I got was static. Wyatt showed up with an armload of twigs and branches and I told him that I couldn't get through to the ship.

"That's strange," he said. "I tested the radios before we left the ship. Let me try mine."

Wyatt tried his radio, too, but he got the same. Static. He checked his GPS and it wasn't working either. There's been all kinds of thunder rumbling overhead and Wyatt thinks that maybe the electricity in the storm is scrambling the signals or something.

"Forget the radios for now and get that fire going," I finally said. "I need to thaw out."

We both sat underneath the tarp, cold and shivering, while Wyatt went about starting a fire. Or attempting to start a fire, I should say. The rainforest is so wet it makes the otherwise simple task of starting a campfire really hard and despite Wyatt's best efforts, he couldn't get one going. Match after match burned to the end and went out without as much as a glowing ember in the pit. I could tell his patience was wearing thin, so, naturally, I made a joke.

"How many *Wyatts* does it take to start a campfire?"

Wyatt turned to me, his jaw rippling as he waited on my punch line.

"Obviously more than one, bro."

"If you're such an expert," he yelled, veins bulging from his neck, "why don't you try to start a fire?"

"Fine," I said. "Step aside and I'll show you how it's done."

I reached into my backpack, removed a Quick-Light Fire Starter (never leave home without one), lit it, tossed it into the kindling, blew softly to fan the flame, and just like that, we had a warm, crackling fire.

Voila!

"Ah, this really warms the old digits," I said wiggling my fingers over the flames.

"Don't talk to me right now," Wyatt said and went about changing into a dry set of clothes.

Here's the problem: I only brought one fire starter. And it's in the fire. I thought there were more in my kit, but when I searched for another, I realized there aren't. It's supposed to get colder after the storm, so if we're not back to the ship tomorrow before nightfall we're going to be in deep trouble.

WYATT

SEPTEMBER 22, 1:47 AM
PRINCESS ROYAL ISLAND (UNABLE TO TAKE COORDINATES)
9° CELSIUS, 49° FAHRENHEIT
CLOUDY WITH A STEADY WIND

Okay, so I broke the third law of exploration. I'm not properly equipped. What kind of explorer sets off into a rainforest without everything he needs to start a fire? I'm so angry with myself I can hardly stand it, and Gannon acting like a know-it-all only makes it worse.

I've been shivering most of the night. Chilled to the bone. I changed out of my wet clothes and have been sitting close to the fire, but this cold damp air is making it impossible to warm up.

Since dark, the rainforest has been alive with noises. Buzzing and screeching and gruffs and howls. Fortunately, we've had no visitors. None that I have seen, anyway.

Okay, just glanced at my expedition watch. It's time for Gannon's shift.

GANNON
MIDDLE OF THE NIGHT

This so-called predator watch has to be the most boring job ever. I'm not even sure why we need to keep watch in the first place. I mean, really, what are we going to do if a pack of wolves comes waltzing into camp? Fight them off with our pocketknives? It would probably be better if we both just slept. The predators are more likely to ignore us that way, and I'll be honest, if a grizzly does materialize out of the darkness I'll probably let out a scream that would shake the needles off a Sitka spruce. And what's that going to do but get us both mauled?

Oh, jeez, what was that?

Something's moving out there.

I can hear leaves rustling. Branches cracking.

This is crazy!

We've burned all the dry wood we collected and the fire is down to a few small flames, but I'm sure as heck not going out to look for more. Not when there's something lurking out there in the darkness. I've got the flashlight next to me, but I'm way too scared to turn it on. I'd probably see twenty glowing eyes right in front of me and there's no way I could handle that. I'd keel over with a heart attack for sure. Definitely keeping the flashlight off. I'd rather not know what's out there watching me.

WYATT

5:56 AM
7° CELSIUS, 46° FAHRENHEIT
CLOUDY, WINDS CALM

At 4:00 AM sharp, Gannon got me up for the final shift.

"This predator watch just about drove me insane," he said, slipping into his sleeping bag. "So, don't wake me until it's light. And by the way, there are all sorts of animals walking around our camp. I suggest you keep your flashlight off. If you shine it in their eyes, it'll probably just provoke an attack. Okay then, I'm going to catch some Zs. Enjoy your shift."

At that he pulled the sleeping bag up over his head. Within a minute he was asleep. Within two minutes, he was snoring.

I had to keep hitting him and plugging his nose and doing whatever I could to stop him. The kid sounded like a wild boar rummaging his snout through the mud. I thought for sure the wolves would come running to devour him, if not for the meal he would provide, then just to shut him up so they could have some peace and quiet.

I took Gannon's advice, put the flashlight away, and sat still next to the dying fire. After adding some wet pine needles and twigs, I stoked the fire and after a while brought back a small flame. The wet clothes I had left on the rocks to dry were still damp. I moved them closer to the pit, hoping the renewed fire would dry them before morning.

Staying dry is critical. Even in September, temperatures at this latitude can drop below freezing. Add wet clothes to the mix and hypothermia becomes a serious threat.

A dim light is just now penetrating the dense canopy overhead. A thin mist floats upward through the trees. The noises that have persisted throughout the night are silent.

Wow! A bald eagle just leapt from a branch and flew directly over our camp. A tremendous "swoosh" could be heard with each flap of the eagle's powerful wings, which must have had a span of six feet or more. What a beautiful creature!

My superstitious brother would probably say that an eagle flying over our camp was a sign of good luck. I hope it is. We need some luck to find everyone and get back to the ship safely. A lot of it.

The majestic bald eagle

GANNON

When we set out this morning, I was whipped and my head was in a fog and I felt totally uncoordinated as we hiked and was pretty much just staggering down this bear path with my eyes half-closed when we came to a wide tributary. On the other side was a field of sedge grass and in the grass just up from the bank of the river was a family of grizzly bears, a mother and two cubs.

You can tell a grizzly from a black bear by the hump located between a grizzly's front shoulders, and these were grizzlies, that's for sure. We were upwind from them and it didn't take long for the mother to pick up our scent. Obviously, the mama griz wasn't too thrilled about us being around and stood up on her hind legs to check us out. Talk about intimidating!

"Don't make any sudden movements," Wyatt whispered.

"Yeah, no kidding," I said.

A mother grizzly can be really aggressive if she thinks her cubs are in danger. Remembering what Alu had taught us, Wyatt and I crouched down and backed away slowly, hoping she would understand that we didn't mean them any harm. I guess she got the message because pretty soon she settled down and went back to eating, uprooting long stalks of grass with her powerful jaws. Once she had a good mouthful, she'd sit back on her hindquarters and chew with her paws dangling limp over her belly. I didn't know grizzlies eat grass, but Wyatt told me there's protein in the sedge grass here and the bears apparently love it. Her cubs didn't seem too interested in eating, though. Instead they wrestled, smacking each other with their paws and rolling around playfully on the shore.

Grizzly cubs love to play

After a while, they tired themselves out. Now they're just lounging around near the stream not doing a whole lot. To watch these bears, even when they're doing nothing, is totally mesmerizing. I just wish I had my video camera with me. This footage would be epic, but as a rule you only bring the essentials on a search and rescue mission, so I'm just resting against the rocks and taking it all in.

WYATT
9:52 AM

Looking through the binoculars gave me a good idea of just how big a grizzly can be. The mother bear's paws were probably the size of a kid's baseball mitt. Her claws were every bit as impressive, extending three full inches from her paw. She was lean, with strong muscular legs that bowed out slightly at the lower half. Her coat was long and light brown. Her two cubs had slightly darker coats and were probably a third her size.

We were about to continue our hike when we noticed the mother's attention turn upstream. All of a sudden she looked disturbed, snorting and nodding her head. Following her line of sight, I saw why. A massive male grizzly had lumbered out of the woods and was crossing the stream. Sometimes the strongest male grizzlies will attack and kill the cubs of other males, a survival instinct that ensures its genes carry on the grizzly bloodline, and not the genes of a weaker male.

Mother grizzly assessing threat of male

The mother grizzly was agitated by the approaching male. He was definitely a threat to the cubs. She knew this and as soon he came across the stream the mother bear charged.

Both bears went up on their hind legs, swinging their immense paws at one another. Even though she was smaller, the female fought hard and seemed to be holding her own. Then the male caught her under the jaw with a powerful blow. She fell backward into the water, rolled onto her side, and struggled to get back to her feet. The male ran after the cubs.

"Run!" Gannon yelled to the cubs. "Run!"

The cubs didn't need to be told. They saw the male bear coming and took off for the cover of the woods.

"Go! Go! Go!" he kept shouting.

"Shut up, Gannon!" I said. "You're going to attract the male's attention and then he's going to come after us!"

"Sorry," Gannon said. "I can't help it."

Again on her feet, the panicked mother ran after them. When the male stopped just short of the forest, she attacked him again. Even more ferocious than the first attack, the mother was willing to fight to the death to protect her cubs.

Gannon was like a diehard boxing fan cheering on his favorite heavyweight fighter.

"Give it to him, mama bear!" he whispered through clinched teeth. "That's it! Don't let him get your babies! Show him who's boss!"

This time the male wanted none of it. He knocked the

mother away with another hard jab before walking back across the creek. The mother limped along the edge of the forest looking for her cubs, growling into the woods in the hope that they would hear her call. I started to worry that she would never find them. If the cubs got lost in the forest, their chance of survival would be slim. Then, suddenly, the cubs appeared at the far end of the sedge field. The mother ran to them and they all tumbled around in the grass. I honestly don't know that I've ever seen such a happy reunion. The bear's affection, I think, is further proof that certain animal species really do experience love.

GANNON
MID-MORNING

Not wanting to cross paths with the grizzlies, we hiked in the opposite direction and followed the path along the shoreline and had been going for about an hour or so when we found Mom and Dad's tender anchored in shallow water just off a sandy beachhead. Oh, man, seeing their boat rocking back and forth in the cove gave me a lump in my throat and a knot in my stomach. I took this huge breath and yelled out as loud as I could:

"Mom! Dad! Can you hear me?"

I kept this up until I was hoarse.

There was no response.

Wyatt and I waded into the cold water to check out the

boat. All of the supplies were gone. So were the keys. It was totally empty, which makes us think they came ashore, but we've found no other sign of them anywhere. No footprints. No clues. Nothing!

Wyatt tried to radio Liam.

"Wyatt to Pacific Yellowfin," he said. "Come in, Pacific Yellowfin. We found the second tender."

Again, there was only static.

"I can't understand this," Wyatt said. "I've tried every channel, but no radio transmissions are getting through."

Frustrated, I picked up a rock and chucked it into the woods.

"None of this adds up," I said. "I'm telling you, there's something strange going on. Four people just don't vanish into thin air without a single call for help."

"What are you saying?" Wyatt asked.

"All I'm saying is that I wouldn't be surprised if Dr. Brezner has something to do with all of this."

"Would you get that absurd idea out of your head?" Wyatt yelled. "I'm tired of hearing it. Our parents are missing and you're trying to place blame. What good does that do? This is a huge wilderness. People go missing in the wilderness all the time! It happens!"

"You have your theory and I have mine!" I shouted back. "I'm not going to argue right now! Bottom line, we have a decision to make!"

And we did. A big one. Continue our search or return to the ship?

Being able to talk to Joe and Liam would be helpful. I mean, the Coast Guard might be en route. Maybe a search is under way. Heck, for all we know, our parents could have been rescued already. Alone on this island with radios that don't work, we have no way of knowing what's going on and that's driving me crazy. Then again, if our parents have been rescued wouldn't they have already returned to pick up the tender? It's this assumption that makes me think we have no choice but to keep searching.

WYATT
11:47 AM

With the hope that our parents were near, we hiked away from the cove. Soon our path along the shore became impassable and we moved inland. We're tired and have stopped to rest and eat. I'm still having a hard time getting my bearings on this island. My GPS has been useless. I'm hoping to spot a geographical landmark, such as Whalen or Butedale Lake, so I can place us on the map because it's pretty much impossible to pinpoint our location in this dense forest. Even along the last stretch of coastline, one cove looked a lot like the next.

All this hiking has been more strenuous than we thought and we've already gone through most of our food. We're down to one last energy bar and a bag of beef jerky. We're going to ration what's left, but if we're on this island much longer, we'll have to catch a salmon or collect mussels. A good meal will be needed to keep our energy up. Our canteens are also close to empty, but there's plenty of fresh water on this island so that's not a problem. After this break, we'll continue our trek in the hopes of finding everyone . . . alive!

A wolf print in the sand

GANNON

LOCATION: NO CLUE!

Our situation is becoming more serious by the minute. I haven't wanted to admit it to Wyatt, but I can write it in my journal:

We're lost!

Earlier, we made a big mistake when we wandered away from the shoreline and into the forest and now we can't find our way out. We've been trying like crazy to make it back to the kayaks for the past two hours, but my guess is that we're farther away from them than we've ever been.

An unknown location in the GBR

I mean, other than the tender, our search has turned up nothing, nada, zilch. There's just no way to put a positive spin on things at this point. Our mission, so far, has been a total and complete failure.

Okay, I admit I'm tired. Aggravated. Cold. Grumpy. My feet and legs are aching. In all honesty, I don't think I could feel worse. So maybe I'm being overly critical, but I just have to get something off my mind so I can focus on the crisis at hand.

Okay, here it is: my brother is driving me nuts.

I know he's a smart kid and aces most of his tests and his IQ is some ridiculously high number and all, but he definitely needs to brush up on his map reading skills. Fine, I'm no good at reading maps either, but I never said I was. I even reminded Wyatt that we needed to stay within eyesight of the coastline during our search, but he wouldn't listen and kept looking at his map and leading us deeper and deeper into the forest. This is a big island and Joe and Liam said that you can get lost real easy. Well, they were right.

For whatever reason, Wyatt keeps studying the map, but it's totally useless. I mean, he may as well be trying to translate Greek.

"What did you bring that map for anyway?" I asked. "You can't even read it!"

"Yes I can!" Wyatt said angrily. "We're about a half mile from the kayaks."

"That's what you said a half mile ago."

"Just keep your mouth shut and follow me!"

I knew we should have radioed Alu before we left the ship. Maybe she would've come with us. I'll fess up, that's totally my fault. I was so anxious to get to the island and find everyone that I just couldn't wait. Now I realize that was a bad call. Alu would have kept us from getting lost. And not only that, she probably would have been able to help us find everyone. But thanks to me, we're all alone and being alone in this tangled, mountainous forest, well, we're pretty much helpless. I mean, I hate to say this and all, but I'm beginning to worry we may never get off this island.

PART III

THE SECRETS OF
PRINCESS ROYAL ISLAND

WYATT

The FOURTH LAW OF EXPLORATION reminds us to document all findings. This is especially true when important discoveries are made, so here's the latest:

After several hours of aimless hiking, we came to a place where the trees were mangled, bent inland, or snapped in half, leading me to believe we'd arrived on the western shore, where violent storms first hit Princess Royal Island. Moving through the tree cover, a large cove came into view. At the far end of the cove, we spotted two fishing boats trolling around the mouth of a river. Gannon immediately slid down the hillside and ran onto the beach, waving his arms around frantically.

"Hey!" he yelled. "Over here! Please help us!"

I caught up with him as fast as I could.

"They're too far away to hear you," I said.

"Then let's hurry and get to the other side before they leave. They'll be able to take us back to the Pacific Yellowfin."

Before I got another word in, Gannon took off around the cove. I followed. As we plowed through the bushes, the sharp spines of Devil's Club sliced my face like tiny razors. Sweat poured down my forehead, stinging the fresh cuts. My legs and stomach were cramping, but I managed to keep up. By the time we reached the other side, I felt like my lungs were about to burst.

The sharp-edged stems of the Devil's Club plant

"Let's get down there!" Gannon yelled, anxiously. "They'll be able to see us from the shore!"

"Wait," I said, panting. "Something isn't right."

"There are two boats in the cove. Either of them can save us. What could possibly be wrong with that?"

"But what are they doing here?" I asked.

"Who cares?"

"Just give me your binoculars."

The captain had said, other than the random sailboat, it was unlikely that we would see another vessel in this area. So what would two fishing boats be doing in protected waters? It just didn't make sense.

Leaning against a rock, I caught my breath and looked through the binoculars. The fishing boats were idling just off shore, one on either side of a wide river. There were two men hustling around the back of each boat. The water between the boats was choppy, as if a current from the sea was colliding with the flow of the river.

"What's going on, Wyatt?"

I didn't answer, only because I didn't have an answer.

"If you don't tell me," he said, "I'm going to run down there and make sure they don't leave without us."

"Give me another minute. I need to get a closer look."

"Fine, I'll give you sixty seconds. Then I'm going with or without you."

We climbed down a muddy slope to a boulder field near the shore.

"Stay low. I don't want them to spot us."

From the shore, I had a clear view. Stretched between

the boats I could see a large fishing net. Trapped inside was a massive school of salmon.

"It's an illegal fishing operation," I said to Gannon.

At any given moment, there were hundreds of salmon jumping through the air, each one trying desperately to make it upriver to spawn. Some of them managed to leap over the net, but most were stuck.

A third man exited the cabin of the boat closest to us and started shouting orders at the others. His voice traveled over the water and sounded oddly familiar. I focused the binoculars to see if I could make out the shadowy figure. When he returned to the cabin a bulb above the door cast a beam of light across his face.

I knew that I recognized the voice.

It was the voice of Dr. Hans Brezner.

Everything Gannon told me about his files raced through my mind. Could he actually be responsible for what was happening on the island?

"That's Dr. Brezner, isn't it?" Gannon asked.

I nodded.

"I told you he was up to no good, Wyatt!"

"We still don't know that for sure."

At the far end of the cove, just off the point, a bright light flashed two times quickly. It must have come from a lookout, someone they had stationed at the point to keep watch for the Coast Guard. The fishing boats returned the signal, two quick bursts of light. Soon after, their engines revved and the boats started for the open ocean. Sadly, thousands of salmon caught in the nets were being dragged with them.

As they turned north, I saw Captain Colin standing at the helm of one of the boats.

"The captain's alive!" I said, excitedly.

"Well, that's a huge relief," Gannon said. "But what's he doing mixed up in all this?"

Taking another look, I saw that the man next to him was holding a gun. It was pointed at the captain.

"He's being held at gunpoint," I said.

Gannon fell back against the rock and let out a sigh.

Again, Dr. Brezner's stern voice carried over the water.

"Sounds to me like Dr. Brezner is in charge of this whole operation," Gannon said.

"Stop jumping to conclusions."

"Come on, Wyatt. You admire the guy and you're letting that cloud your judgment. I think he's involved, whether you want to admit it or not. And if that's true, he's probably responsible for Mom and Dad's disappearance!"

"That's enough!" I shouted. "I don't want to hear anymore!"

Frustrated, Gannon stood and walked off.

"You're so stubborn sometimes," he said, as he climbed over the rocks. "I'm heading back around the cove. You can catch up whenever you feel like it."

What bothers me most is that Gannon's accusations have some merit. The doctor's involvement is definitely suspicious.

I can't make heads or tails of what's going on. I wonder if they are netting the salmon at the mouths of other rivers, too. I wonder if these men are responsible for the low salmon numbers Alu observed last season. I wonder just how damaging a large-scale netting operation would be to the Great Bear Rainforest. It's as if they are trying to sabotage the entire ecosystem. Why would someone do such a thing? For the life of me, I just can't understand it.

GANNON
LATE AT NIGHT

When Wyatt caught up with me we called a truce and went looking for something to eat near the shore so we could keep the last of the food we'd brought for morning. It was pretty dark with only a little moonlight coming through the clouds and that made the search pretty difficult, but eventually I came across a shallow pool in the rocks that was full of mussels. We stuffed our jacket pockets and rinsed them in a nearby stream before taking cover in the woods to eat. With our pocketknives we cracked open the shells, tore away the beards and slurped down the slimy mussels. They were all rubbery and salty and would have been hard for me to stomach under normal circumstances, but we were so hungry we swallowed them one after another and soon my hunger pains went away.

After eating, we tramped back into the dark and looked

for a place to stay the night. By total luck we found this narrow little cave under a steep rock face, a couple hundred feet up from the beach. We're now settled into a nook within the cave where the ground is dry, so we figure it's pretty well protected from the rain and not a place where a flash flood might wash us away.

Tonight it's going to be a challenge to stay warm. I mean, I'm already cold and have my jacket zipped up over my mouth and I'm breathing into it to fill the area around my body with warm air. That's all the warmth I'm going to get because there isn't enough ventilation in this cave to start a fire, and even if we wanted to start one it'd be nearly impossible in this cold, wet place, being out of fire starters and all.

When I opened my journal, I thought that making some notes on our camp might occupy my brain for a while, but the fear of being alone on this island and knowing Dr. Brezner is up to no good and the worry that we'll never find my parents and the fact that we have no way to call for help, well, all these things are just eating me up inside.

I desperately need some sleep.

WYATT
SEPTEMBER 23, 8:43 AM

After a frigid night in the cave, we finished off the last of our food and set out before first light. My whole body aches. My face is scraped up and welted from insect bites. My mouth is dry. My lips are cracked and bleeding. We need to find a good stream and drink. Worst, I can't stop thinking about my parents. I even dreamt about them last night. We have to find them. Have to. But that's the problem. We're lost.

Neither of us feels much like talking right now. Really, there is nothing more to say.

GANNON

Well, this sure is interesting. We've stumbled upon a small camp. Kind of looks like an army barrack with a few tents all covered in moss and tree limbs and stuff. Two men are standing around outside and it looks like they have guns. We're pretty high above the camp, hidden behind some trees. Planning to go in for a closer look. Our parents could be down there!

WYATT
SEPTEMBER 23, 10:52 AM

We've been spotted!

We're on the run!

Two gunmen are after us!

We've lost them for now, but I know they're still coming. They wouldn't give up that easily. I'm writing just in case anything should happen to us. I'm writing for my parents, for the authorities, or whoever might find this journal. There's so much to tell, but we have to keep moving . . .

GANNON

We hadn't seen the gunmen in a while and I was begging Wyatt to stop because my legs were about to buckle and my heart was beating out of my chest and I needed to catch my breath. We found a good flowing stream coming out of the mountains and stopped to drink and wash our faces and rest along the bank. I hid myself behind a rock and looked around. Everything was still the same—the forest and mountains and rocky coast, everything! It seemed more likely than ever that we'd be on this island for the rest of our lives, not that that would have been long given the way we were going, then, just like that, our luck took a turn.

We left the stream and were heading north, I think, and trying to keep as close to the shore as we could with the hope that we would somehow avoid the gunmen and miraculously stumble upon the kayaks and paddle back to the Pacific Yellowfin and be saved, when I caught sight of something moving through the trees. I pulled Wyatt down behind some bushes.

"Stay down," I said. "Someone's coming."

"Where?"

"Up ahead."

"Is it the gunmen?"

"I don't know."

When I looked through my binoculars, I couldn't believe my eyes.

It was Alu!

The way she moved through the forest, making it look so effortless, it was almost like she was on a stroll in her own backyard. Wyatt and I both ran from the bushes as fast as we could and yanked her down behind some rocks.

"Sorry for scaring you, Alu," Wyatt whispered, "But we have to stay out of sight. We're being chased by two armed men."

"Two armed men?" she repeated, confused.

"How in the world did you find us, Alu?" I whispered.

"When I was told you both left the boat against Joe's orders, I thought you might need help, so I came to the island and tracked you. On a mountainous island like this, follow the path of least resistance and you will almost always find what you're looking for."

"Have you heard anything about my parents?" Wyatt asked.

"No, I'm sorry," she said. "No word on your parents, but most people believe the captain and Dr. Brezner are dead."

"That's not true," I said. "They're alive. We've seen them."

"You have?"

"Listen," I said, "Dr. Brezner is not who he seems."

"We don't know that," Wyatt argued.

"Okay, fine, I'm not 100% sure, but I think he's somehow involved in my parents' disappearance. Last night we saw a couple fishing boats netting all these salmon at the mouth of some river and Dr. Brezner was on one of the boats shouting orders. Captain Colin was there, too, but it looked like he was being forced to help. Then, this morning we came across a camp hidden in the woods and now we got a couple lunatic gunmen after us."

"My father has always felt that Dr. Brezner was not to be trusted," Alu said.

"Listen," Wyatt said, "can you help us find our parents?"

"Do you think they're in the camp?"

"They might be," Wyatt said, "but we can't go back there unless we're with the Coast Guard. It's too risky."

"The Coast Guard is searching the island, too, but they haven't found anything. Have you come across any clues that could help lead us to them?"

"We found the tender that they took ashore. It's anchored in a cove somewhere on the eastern side of the island."

"Describe the cove to me. We'll track from there."

We've taken shelter under a fallen tree and are waiting for the rain to let up and for the first time in a long time I'm actually hopeful. I mean, now that we're with Alu, our chances of finding our parents and getting off this island alive are a whole lot better and thank goodness for that because the alternative isn't so desirable.

WYATT
11:43 AM

It had stopped raining and we were about to continue our trek when we spotted something moving through the forest

115

below. Looking through the binoculars, our worst fear was realized. It was the gunmen!

Before we had time to react, one of the men saw us, put his rifle to his shoulder, and fired. A bullet cut through the trees overhead. We took cover and the men started up the hill after us. Our only option was to climb higher, away from the gunmen. We scrambled around the fallen trees and continued moving up the mountain until we reached a granite cliff face. We would need ropes to climb any higher and the gunmen were gaining on us.

"What do we do?" Gannon asked in a panic.

There was only one thing we could do.

"We have to get across this cliff," I said.

"I agree," Alu said. "Otherwise, we'll be captured."

"I don't think we can make it," Gannon said.

"We have to try."

There was a large split in the rock, about four-feet high and three-feet deep, where the mountain had fractured. It formed a small ledge that ran the length of the cliff face. Alu thought that we could escape the gunmen by crawling along this ledge to the other side where there was a much gentler slope. It would be risky, but we had no other choice.

"That's a long way to fall," Gannon said, looking down.

"Don't look down," Alu said. "Stay focused."

Below the ledge was a smooth and sheer slab of granite that eventually fell so steeply it dropped completely out of sight. A river ran through the valley about 300-vertical feet from where we stood.

"We have to go," Alu said, frantically. "They're getting closer!"

She led the way, moving along the ledge like a mountain goat. I followed, wedging myself as deeply into the rock as I could, knowing that one simple misstep might send me plummeting to my death. I was so afraid I honestly didn't know if I would be able to move.

"You okay, Wyatt?" Gannon asked.

"I think so," I said, "I just need a minute."

"Try to relax," Alu yelled from up ahead. "The ledge actually gets wider as you go. Crawl forward slowly. Stay focused and we'll all make it."

I tried, but it was impossible to keep from looking down. Out of the corner of my eye, I could see the granite slope falling sharply into the valley below. The wide river looked like a tiny stream from that height. My heart raced. My palms were damp. I looked down at the cold, gray rock underneath my hands and could not move. Sweat dripped steadily from my nose. I took deep breaths, trying to settle my nerves and keep from shaking. Finally, I was able to put one hand forward and begin moving across the cliff.

Gannon followed.

Cautiously, we crawled across the ledge, making slow progress toward the other side. The gunmen gave up on the climb when they saw us traversing the rock face. They were far below and stopped to watch, probably thinking we would never make it to the other side.

The sound of sliding dirt and gravel jolted me to a stop. When I turned around, I saw my brother lying on his stomach, his legs hanging over the ledge. Underneath him, several rocks tumbled down the slope and disappeared over the cliff. His arms were spread out, his palms pressed against the rock. There was nothing for him to hold on to.

"Stay still, Gannon!" I yelled. "I'm coming!"

Carefully, I reversed my direction and began crawling toward him.

There wasn't enough friction between Gannon and the rock to hold him steady. Too much loose gravel and dirt. He began to slip.

"Wyatt," he said, terrified, "please, help me."

"I'll be right there."

"Hang on, Gannon!" Alu yelled. "You can do it!"

Gannon was trying with all his might to brace himself. His body was shaking, almost convulsing at the effort. Despite this, he kept inching lower.

"I can't hang on much longer," he said.

"Yes you can!" Alu shouted.

"Just give me another few seconds," I said, scrambling across the ledge as quickly as I could.

"I'm slipping!" he yelled.

I lunged and grabbed his jacket. Gannon stopped sliding. I had him.

For a moment, I lay flat on the rock, not wanting to make any movement that might weaken my grip. Then, slowly, I moved to my knees. Once I had my legs under me, I was able to pull him higher.

But Gannon's weight proved too much for the jacket to support. Before I could pull him safely onto the ledge, his zipper broke and the jacket opened. He was about to come out of it completely.

"Quick!" I said, "Grab my hand!"

Gannon reached up and took my hand. Both of our palms were sweaty. It was hard to get a grip. No matter how hard I pulled, Gannon kept slipping.

"Be strong, Gannon!" Alu yelled, crawling back across the ledge toward us.

"Don't let go of me, Wyatt," Gannon pleaded.

"I won't, Gannon. You're not going to fall. I've got you."

I thought I was going to bust a blood vessel in my head, I was pulling so hard. It didn't matter. I wasn't about to let my brother fall to his death.

Truth is, gravity was winning the battle.

Gannon's hand continued to slip through mine. I tried to tighten my grip, but his hand only slipped further.

Gannon lifted his head, stared at me, a look of disbelief in his eyes.

"Don't let me fall," he whispered. "Please."

"You won't fall," I said, staring back at him. "I've got you!"

It was a promise.

A promise I could not keep.

My grip was giving way.

"No," I said, through clinched teeth. "Nooooo!"

Gannon's hand slipped from mine.

I reached again for his jacket but missed. He was sliding, trying desperately to grab hold of anything that might stop him. He dug his fingers into the rock, but nothing would break his fall.

Our eyes met one last time.

A horrific scream erupted from his lungs as he slid over the cliff, out of sight.

His scream trailed off.

There was silence.

My brother was gone.

I'm not sure how I functioned after Gannon's fall. Alu must have taken over. I was overcome with grief. Completely lost. All I could see were Gannon's eyes just before his hand slipped from mine. All I heard was the terror in his voice. It echoed inside my head, repeated itself over and over. I had the chance to save him and I failed.

Awful thoughts plagued me every step of the way. How will I tell Mom and Dad? How will they react? That is, if we ever find them. They could be dead, too!

I was living a nightmare.

I tried to think practically. We needed to find Gannon's body. We needed to get him back to the ship. How we were going to do it, I had no idea, but I wasn't about to leave him in the forest. I would carry him on my back if I had to.

Alu guided us down the mountain to the river. We combed

the shoreline that ran along the base of the cliff, looking in and around the rocks and trees.

I was devastated, shattered. My body numb. Hands trembling. I questioned every decision we had made since leaving the ship. Every single move. All of our missteps.

I looked up the cliff to see if I could locate the spot from which he had fallen, but a dense forest grew along the lower part of the mountain, obscuring my view.

The cliff face

We pushed further down the river and came to a massive set of boulders grouped along the shore. Climbing the largest of these boulders gave us a good, high view of the area.

That's when we found him.

The sight of his body was shocking. My heart fell into my stomach. A lump rose up in my throat, nearly choking off my air. I tried my best to hold it together. The tears came anyway.

There he was, my twin brother, lying on his stomach in a shallow pool near the river's edge. His face was impacted in the mud. Rapids washed up and over the rocks that separated the river from the pool. Any more rain would bring the water up higher and carry him away.

I closed my eyes and cried.

"You did everything you could," Alu said, placing her hand gently on my shoulder. "Gannon knows that."

I couldn't bring myself to speak.

As we moved down the bank toward Gannon's body, I glanced up at him and could have sworn I saw his arm move ever so slightly. I rubbed my eyes and then locked them on Gannon, desperate to see him move again.

Had it really happened?

Suddenly, Gannon lifted his head from the mud. He looked around and put his head back down.

"Did you see that?" I yelled to Alu. "Please tell me you saw that!"

"I did!" she said. "He's alive!"

He was alive! He lifted his head again. This time he looked in our direction. I saw his face. It was bruised and swollen at the eye. Blood poured from a gash on his forehead.

"We're coming, Gannon!" I yelled. "Hang in there! We're coming!"

Gannon wasn't out of danger. Far from it. I was afraid he might be paralyzed or bleeding internally. We had no way of knowing the extent of his injuries. Assuming he was disoriented from the fall, I was also afraid he'd roll over and be swept away by the rapids. We had to get to him right away.

I was climbing as fast as I could up and over the boulders that lined the shore, when I felt something tugging on my jacket.

"Wyatt!" Alu yelled. "Stop!"

"What's the matter?" I said, impatiently.

"Look!" she said, pointing down the river, not far from Gannon.

There, moving in his direction, was a pack of wolves.

"What should we do?" I asked.

As they came nearer to Gannon, the wolves, six in total, worked themselves into a frenzy.

"These wolves will attack if we get in their way," Alu said.

"But we can't just stand here! They'll tear my brother to pieces! We have to do something!"

I picked up a rock and threw it at them, but we were too far away.

"Let's get closer and try to run them off," I said.

"Be careful," Alu warned. "They won't be scared away easily, and they could spring on us in an instant."

I tried to stay hidden behind the fallen tree trunks as we moved down the bank. The wolves continued to close in on Gannon. I picked up a rock the size of a baseball and threw it at the smallest of the wolves. The rock missed. I immediately picked up another and threw this one even harder. The rock found its target, hitting the thin male on the shoulder of his hind leg. Startled, the wolf yelped and turned to us. Half of the pack responded to the wolf's cry and began moving in our direction. The wolf I'd hit with the rock led the pack, hobbling slightly. The remaining wolves were nearly on top of Gannon.

An angry wolf closes in

My intent had been to scare them off, but I had only made the situation worse. There was nothing left to do but defend ourselves. Alu and I threw as many rocks as we could, one after another. Ignoring this hail of stones, the wolves moved closer. They were snarling. Howling. Just ripping mad. Their fangs like razors.

We were facing a gruesome end. There was no way to back them down. I looked around frantically for anything I could use as a weapon, when all of a sudden, something in the forest caught the packs' attention. The wolves' ferocious howls turned to whimpers and they started to back away, cowering as they moved lower along the bank of the river. There was something coming through the trees above us, and whatever it was terrified the wolves. Alu and I looked up the hill to see what had them so scared. Standing atop a boulder, like the king of the rainforest, was a bear. A beautiful, white bear. So rare are sightings, I couldn't believe my eyes. Nevertheless, there it was.

A spirit bear!

The wolves finally scampered off into the forest, and we ran to Gannon's aid. He had rolled over on his own power and was semi-conscious when we got to him, but he still managed a smile when he saw my face. Seeing his smile changed everything for me.

We've moved Gannon away from the river and are waiting for him to come to. Once he's alert, we need to do a more thorough assessment of his injuries. In the meantime, I think I'll go ahead and collapse.

GANNON

How I survived that fall, I'll never know. I guess someone was looking after me. The spirits of the rainforest maybe. At least that's what I like to think. I mean, the last thing I remember was sliding off that huge cliff and crashing through a bunch of trees and after that my mind pretty much went blank. Maybe the trees broke my fall or maybe it was the water and mud where I landed that softened the impact. Who knows? It's all a total blur. What I remember most clearly is the sound of the wolves howling. How it got louder and louder as they came closer. The other thing I remember is the white light coming through the trees. It started out small and then got bigger, intensifying until all I could see was this beaming white light—like some kind of passage to the afterlife. There was no question in my mind: *I was dead!* On my way to that far-off place in the sky! Good-bye, world! Then, next thing I know, I'm lying next to a campfire all wrapped up in a wool blanket with Wyatt and Alu standing over me.

"Where am I?" I asked.

"Princess Royal Island."

"Still?"

"Yes," Wyatt said with a smile. "Still."

Trying to figure out how badly I was injured, Wyatt and Alu asked all kinds of questions and I went about describing what hurt and how bad. I felt kind of dizzy, but I wanted to get up to see how well I could move around, and asked Wyatt and Alu to help. They supported my back and neck as I sat up, and this crazy pain shot through my ribs like a lightning bolt and my entire body seized up, making even the slightest movement so painful I could hardly stand it. The only thing that didn't hurt was my left arm and that's because I couldn't feel it at all. It was all wrapped up below the elbow in some sort of makeshift tourniquet.

"You think it's broken?" I asked.

"It was bent between the elbow and the wrist," Wyatt said. "I'm no physician, but yeah, I'm pretty sure it's broken."

I didn't need to hear anymore.

Needless to say, the fall banged me up pretty good. There is positive news, though. I can walk. I mean, I need lots of help to do it, but I can walk. My right leg is really sore and I think it might be fractured below the knee because I can't really handle much weight on it, but my legs work, they move, and that's no small miracle.

Wyatt and Alu's examination took awhile and totally wore me out and throughout the whole thing their voices seemed to get louder and louder and all of a sudden the pounding in my head got so bad it felt like someone was hammering on my skull with a pickax.

"I have a splitting headache," I said.

"Probably has something to do with the gash on the side of your forehead," Wyatt said. "We patched it up the best we could with a butterfly bandage."

"How big is it?"

"Three, maybe three-and-a-half inches across. And deep.

It'll definitely need proper stitches as soon as we can get you to a doctor."

The thought of stitches made me lightheaded. I hate needles, especially when they're being stuck into my skin.

"I need to rest for a minute," I said, my head woozy.

While Alu piled up wood for a fire, Wyatt put the blanket back over me and propped my head under a rolled up fleece and I closed my eyes and took long, deep breaths and the pain in my head eased up a little and I was actually able to relax. When I opened my eyes there were flames coming off the wood and Alu added some more sticks and the flames grew big and hot and felt really good as they warmed my cold, aching body.

"How'd you get this fire going when everything is so wet?" I asked Alu. "Did you bring fire starters?"

"No," she said, showing off that beautiful smile of hers. "There are other ways. I'll teach you sometime."

"I would love that," I said, almost blushing.

"But for now, you must rest."

Alu cooked a salmon she'd grabbed from the river and passed steaming chucks of pink meat to us, while Wyatt told the crazy story of my rescue and how a spirit bear had suddenly appeared out of nowhere and saved my life.

"That explains the white light I remember seeing," I said.

"Here's what I don't understand," Wyatt said. "A spirit bear, no matter how big, is no match for a pack of wolves."

"That's true," Alu said.

"So why did the wolves back away when the spirit bear appeared?"

"I can't say for sure. Some people believe the spirit bear is the guardian of the forest. A protector of all things good and righteous in the Great Bear. Maybe it is true."

Wyatt quietly pondered what Alu had said.

A spirit bear, up close and personal

Now, my brother is the kind of person who needs a scientific explanation for everything. Fact is, a pack of wolves could kill a spirit bear, so why didn't they? Here's the problem: mythical explanations, like Alu's, can't really be proven, scientifically speaking, so Wyatt's always quick to dismiss this kind of stuff as untrue. That's why it's so strange that he didn't. With his own eyes, he'd seen something unexplainable, something magical. Crazy as it sounds, I think for the first time in his life my brother could be open to the possibility that some things might just be greater than science.

WYATT
2:37 PM

The FIFTH LAW OF EXPLORATION is the most important of all the laws. It states, simply: Live to explore another day.

We've almost broken this law several times since arriving in the Great Bear. That being said, we're still alive. I believe my parents are still alive, too. Maybe they got lost somewhere on the island, like us. Maybe they were captured by the gunmen and are being held at the camp. Whatever happened, one thing is for sure, they're in need of rescue.

Like a mantra, I keep repeating the fifth law in my head. We need to be smart. Poor decision making has put us in danger, and it's only luck that has kept us alive. It's my fault for making decisions without considering all of the possible outcomes. But I learn from my mistakes and I'm not about to let us take any more unnecessary risks.

We thought about sending Alu back to her boat so she could get to the Pacific Yellowfin for help but decided it's best we stay together. We also considered trekking back into the interior of the island to look for my parents and returning to Gannon before nightfall, but even with Alu to guide us, that wouldn't be smart. She's confident she could track our parents and I'm sure she could. Finding them isn't what concerns me. My concern is the gunmen.

If we're going to take them down and find my parents, we need the help of professionals. We need the Canadian Coast Guard!

GANNON

I've begged and pleaded for Wyatt and Alu to leave me here and go find our mom and dad or get back to the ship and bring help because every minute counts and we can't just sit here doing nothing, but they won't listen to me. They think it's best we all stay put and try to signal for help and I'm outvoted, so I guess that's that.

Alu got the campfire going again with all kinds of leaves and branches and a real dark smoke started floating off the fire and while I was lying there watching her toss sticks onto the flame, this crazy dream I had after my fall came rushing back into my brain.

In the dream, Wyatt and I were on the island, somewhere deep in the forest and we were building a fire, just like Alu, and for some reason I insisted that we add a specific type of tree branch to the flames. Not sure how, but I knew exactly what I was looking for and soon found the tree, a smallish type evergreen, no taller than me. With Wyatt's ax,

I chopped off several branches thick with pine needles and went back to the fire saying something to Wyatt about the branches being poisonous and warning him not to inhale the smoke or he would get dizzy or nauseous or worse. After tying bandanas over our noses and mouths and moving upwind, we threw the poisonous branches on the fire. A thick and potent smoke rose off the flames and drifted into the forest.

Anyway, that's where the dream ended. Now, I believe that most dreams have some kind of meaning. But if this dream has a meaning, I don't have the slightest clue what it is.

The fire is really blazing now and Alu is whipping the tarp around to make these little clouds of black smoke, three at a time.

"Three puffs of smoke means someone is in distress," she explained. "Hopefully, Joe and Liam will see the smoke and send help."

"But what if the gunmen see the smoke?" I asked.

"We have to take that chance. There is no other way to call for help."

Fingers crossed the wrong people don't see our smoke signals. If they do, we're done for.

WYATT
5:12 PM

I thought we would be here for hours, or even days, before

anyone saw our smoke signal, but a boat just came around the point at the end of the cove and is headed our way!

I can hardly believe it!

It's the Canadian Coast Guard!

We're saved!

I wonder if they've already found my parents, the captain, and Dr. Brezner? If not, at least they are on the case. With the Coast Guard involved, it's only a matter of time.

They're pulling up to shore.

Will give an update later. . . .

GANNON

A bright red zodiac boat came drifting onto the beachhead and five Coast Guard officers jumped out. The man in charge said his name was Officer Briggs and he went around checking to make sure that no one was in any immediate danger. Of course, I'm the worst off and before I knew what was happening a couple medics were hovering over me, shining lights in my eyes and cleaning my wounds with alcohol swabs and wrapping up my arm in a soft cast.

"It's a relief to see that you are okay, Alu," Officer Briggs said, placing his hand on her shoulder.

"You know I can hold my own in the forest," Alu said.

"You two know each other?" Wyatt asked.

"Alu's father was just hired to help train the Coast Guard officers in the Great Bear Rainforest."

"The Coast Guard was smart to hire someone like my father," Alu said with a modest smile. "Is he worried about me?"

"Of course he's worried. You should have told someone exactly where you were going."

"I'm sorry," Alu said. "I just thought I'd come alone and try to figure out what had happened before I troubled anyone."

"We tried to radio for help," Wyatt explained, "but our radios haven't worked since we got to the island."

"Something is jamming the frequencies," Officer Briggs said. "When we're on the island, our radios don't work either."

Officer Briggs said that we were the first of the missing to be found and that no one else had been heard from since leaving the Pacific Yellowfin. Wyatt told the Coast Guard about the fishing boats and the camp and the gunmen and how they fired at us and how we went up the cliff and all that. I thought about explaining my theory that Dr. Brezner was in charge of the whole operation and responsible for everyone's disappearance, but I decided that opening my mouth would only start an argument with Wyatt and that wouldn't get us anywhere.

Officer Briggs decided that he and two other officers would set off on foot in search of the gunmen or the camp, assuming that if they found one or the other, it would lead them to everyone else. The two other officers would take me back to the Pacific Yellowfin, where they could do a full medical examination and call in an airlift to the hospital, if necessary. They asked Alu to be part of the search team, seeing as how she knows the island as well as anyone. Wyatt insisted he be allowed to go, too, but Officer Briggs wasn't sure that was a good idea.

"You have to let me go with you," Wyatt pleaded. "My parents are out there. They've been missing for a few days now. I won't be able to rest until I know what's happened to them. Besides, Gannon and I are the only ones who have seen the camp. I can lead us there. I know I can."

Officer Briggs thought for a moment and finally agreed to let Wyatt join the expedition. Right away the men went to work preparing for the mission, strapping on their packs and checking their equipment and, most important, making sure their weapons were locked and loaded. I mean, there's no doubt in anyone's mind, a showdown with the gunmen is almost certain.

I wanted so badly to be going with them. I wanted to be there to protect my brother if anything happens. I wanted to help them find my parents. But, obviously, that just wasn't in the cards for me.

After they put me on the boat, I lifted my head from the stretcher and watched the search party climb the rocks and move back toward the forest. Bravely leading the way was my brother.

Just before they disappeared into the trees this crazy idea sprang to mind. I yelled to Alu:

"Are there any poisonous trees in this forest?"

"Yes!" Alu yelled back. "Several!"

"Is there one that looks like a small pine tree?"

"There is! It's called a Yew!"

The meaning of my dream struck me like a bolt of lightning.

"If you find the camp," I said, "try smoking them out with the Yew! May sound totally crazy, but the toxins in the smoke might incapacitate the gunmen and that might prevent anyone from getting hurt!"

WYATT

INTERIOR OF PRINCESS ROYAL ISLAND
8:34 PM

Sometimes my brother amazes me. How he came up with the idea to smoke out the camp, I can't even imagine. At first, I thought that he must have bruised his brain during the fall and now thought he was a First Nation medicine man.

I asked Alu what she thought of his plan.

"I think it might actually work," she said.

"Are you serious?" I asked, totally shocked.

"I honestly think it might."

"I wonder how he knew about the poisonous tree?"

"I believe the spirits have spoken to Gannon. They have shown him the way."

Spirits?

Well, I'm not so sure about all that, but I held my tongue. There has to be a logical explanation. There always is. Then again, I've witnessed some strange things in this forest, things that don't seem to have a logical explanation. One thing I can't deny, the Great Bear Rainforest is a mysterious place.

Within the first ten minutes of the trek, we came across a Yew tree and filled an entire backpack with its branches. I guess Gannon's plan is worth trying. All things considered, it's probably our best option at preventing a shoot out.

Within the first twenty minutes of our trek, I was lost. Tall mountains seemed to be closing in on all sides. I was disoriented and didn't know which way to go. Alu could tell I was lost and several times came to my rescue, raising her arm and pointing to an area of the forest where a trail might be made. At that, the trek would continue.

Daylight was fading. Heavy wind gusts swirled in the trees overhead, making a whooshing sound like waves crashing on the shore. I was struggling to put one foot in front of the other when Alu came across a footprint in the mud. She must have the eyes of a hawk, because the footprint was hardly visible in the dim light.

"One footprint usually leads to another," she said, quietly, and continued ahead.

We did find another, then another, leading up the gulch to a narrow ridgeline, but before we made it to the top more rain came, washing away the rest of the footprints. By the time the front passed through and the rain stopped, it was dark.

Officer Briggs halted the search, so that we could all rest and discuss our options. As we talked, the skies cleared. I glanced up into the trees and noticed a star flickering in the sky, the first star I've seen since we arrived in the Great Bear Rainforest.

The temperature is falling. Mist tumbles from our mouths with each breath. On the low horizon, rising over a distant peak, a full moon sends a soft light through the trees. It's a night that perfectly describes the meaning of our new friend's name—*Alu*!

"On clear nights when the moon is full, travelers are promised safe passage," she said with a smile.

I hope this is true.

If the skies stay clear, it will definitely help our search.

On we go . . .

WYATT
SEPTEMBER 24, 9:57 AM

I wish I could write that it all went perfectly to plan, that we bravely rescued my parents without incident, that I scoffed in the face of death, but it sure didn't go down that way. Truth is, we needed help.

So, here's what happened. We were hiking along under the stars, when Alu stopped us and pointed into the woods.

"Look," she said with excitement in her voice.

About a quarter-mile away, standing next to a tree, was a spirit bear, its white coat glowing in the moonlight like a beacon in the dark forest. The bear stepped around the tree and walked slowly up the hill. When it had climbed to the top of the ridge, the bear stopped and turned back to us.

A spirit bear leads the way

Without saying a word, Alu moved down the slope in the direction of the bear. We all followed her, quickly making it to the bottom of the ravine, and began climbing the opposite slope. When the spirit bear saw that we were moving up the hill toward him, he turned and disappeared over the ridge.

Within a few minutes, we made it to the ridge where we had last seen the bear. There was no sign of him.

"Where did he go?" I asked.

"There," Alu said, pointing.

The spirit bear had traversed a steep slope and was standing at the edge of a rock outcropping. He stood perfectly still, his eyes fixed. Following the bear's line of sight, I noticed something at the base of the valley.

"There it is," I said, tapping Officer Briggs on the shoulder. "The camp."

"Well done," he said. "Let's get closer and assess the situation."

When I looked back to the outcropping, the spirit bear was gone. It almost seemed like he had led us to the camp. Could that be true? I only had a split second to ponder this thought, as Officer Briggs and the others were ready to set out for the camp.

"If we climb up and over these rocks," Officer Briggs said, "we can move down the slope through the trees on the other side. Once we're there, we'll find a safe place for you and Alu to take cover behind the rocks before the men and I move into camp."

Alu followed close behind and I brought up the rear. I stopped and turned back for a moment, hoping to catch sight of my parents somewhere in the camp. I was dying to know that they were okay.

The camp was quiet.

I saw nothing.

The rest of the group moved up a steep gulch and disappeared from sight behind some rocks. I had fallen behind and set out to catch up.

Just as I started the climb, a hand came over my face, clutching my nose and mouth so hard I couldn't breathe. I kicked and squirmed with all my might as I was pulled back down the gulch, but I was in the grasp of someone much stronger and couldn't break free.

The man carried me behind a rock and threw me to the ground, his hand still pressed hard over my face. He was dirty and disheveled, with long shaggy hair and a beard. I immediately recognized him as one of the gunmen. With his free hand he pressed his index finger to his lips and then lowered it.

"If you try to get away," he said, pointing to a gun stuck in his waistband, "it'll be the end for you."

Judging by the looks of this guy, he was more than capable of following through on his threat.

"Get up," he said and yanked me to my feet.

He shoved me and we began marching toward camp. We went down the hillside to an area below the main camp, where a single large camouflage tent had been set up. The gunman pushed me through the door, forced me into a chair, and quickly tied up my hands and feet with rope.

"Don't try anything stupid," he said. "I'll be right back."

At that he gagged me with a bandana and disappeared through the door.

My hands were tied behind my back. With all the strength I could manage, I tried to wiggle them loose. When that didn't work, I leaned forward and tried to pull an arm free. I could feel the skin beginning to tear at my wrist.

Just then, a voice startled me:

"Going somewhere?"

Flanked by the two gunmen, stood Dr. Brezner.

He knelt down and looked me dead in the eyes. His stare sent a chill down my spine. In his eyes, I saw a different Dr. Brezner than the one I had come to know. His eyes seemed to burn right through me, like the eyes of a madman.

"Listen to me," he said, sternly. "When I remove this handkerchief you do not make a sound unless you are answering a question that I have asked. Do you understand?"

I nodded.

Dr. Brezner reached up and removed the gag from my mouth.

"Who else knows the location of our camp?" he asked.

"No one," I said.

"You're alone?" he asked.

Again, I nodded.

"A young boy trekking across this dangerous island on his own. I find that hard to believe."

"It's true."

"I know Alu and your brother were with you!" Dr. Brezner said with agitation in his voice. "Where are they?"

I paused for a moment and took a deep breath. Almost

certain that the gunmen had seen Gannon slide off the cliff, I decided to lie again.

"My brother's dead," I said, somberly. "Alu went back to the ship to get help."

Dr. Brezner looked to his men, who confirmed that they had seen Gannon slip and fall out of sight. Dr. Brezner stared at me, but didn't say a word.

"You don't believe me?" I said, angrily. "It's true. My brother's dead. I tried to save him, but I couldn't. He's dead!"

Having believed this to be true only hours earlier, the emotion came rushing back. Tears welled up in my eyes. My head sank and I cried. It was this bit of unintended acting that convinced Dr. Brezner I was telling the truth.

"It's unfortunate that you had to endure such an experience," he said. "But it wasn't I who brought you onto this island. You assumed that risk on your own."

Dr. Brezner stood and gave instructions to his men.

"Search the perimeter and make sure no one else is with him."

The gunmen left the tent.

"What'd you do to my parents?" I asked, impatiently.

"Never mind your parents, right now," he said. "You'll be joining them soon enough."

"Are they alive?" I asked, horrified.

"For now."

"Why are you doing this?" I said. "Why are you destroying the forest?"

"You're a clever boy, Wyatt. You and Alu were right. There is an explanation as to why so few salmon are making it upriver to spawn."

"Because you're netting them," I said. "We saw your boats in the cove, but I don't understand why you're doing it."

"It's very simple. As you well know, the natural resources in this wilderness are worth billions. The question is, how does one get their hands on them? As long as this area is protected by the Canadian government, it's simply not possible. I was hired to change that."

Dr. Brezner put his hands in his pockets and strolled around the tent casually.

"You see, my clients are impatient people. They don't want to wait around hoping the government will one day have a change of heart. They want the resources in this forest, and they want them now."

"I don't get it," I said, hoping he'd continue.

"The sooner this rainforest ceases to be a vibrant wilderness, the sooner there are no spirit bears to protect, the sooner government protection will be lifted. At that point, a few select companies will be able to extract whatever resources they wish. I am simply speeding up the process by ridding this area of salmon."

"You've betrayed your life's work," I said.

"Wyatt, my dear boy. In my career, I've learned that conservationists may be able to save small areas of wilderness here and there, but the protection will never last. It is only in place until a more powerful group with more money comes along and wants what the earth has to offer. There is no use fighting it."

It was still hard for me to believe that the doctor could suddenly abandon everything he'd believed in for so long.

"So you gave it all up for money?" I asked.

The doctor leaned in, looking me in the eyes.

"For orchestrating this one deed," he said, "I will make enough money to do whatever I wish for the rest of my life, and do so in peace. That is my desire. Now, if you'll excuse me. I have to assist my men in detaining whomever else may have come snooping around with you."

"I told you I was alone," I said.

"You did. But I don't believe you."

"I want to see my parents," I said, trying my best to hold it together. "At least give me that. Please, let me see them!"

As the doctor considered my request, traces of smoke floated through the tent.

"Something is burning," the doctor said as he stuck his head outside the tent.

I knew what was burning. Alu and the Coast Guard had lit the Yew bush and were smoking out the camp with toxic fumes. I took a deep breath and held it.

Dr. Brezner ran outside yelling.

"What's going on here?"

I heard men coughing. I closed my eyes and tried to concentrate. The more relaxed I was, the longer I would be able to hold my breath.

The coughing outside got worse. Someone sounded as if he was gagging. Others were shouting. A man yelled at someone to "get down!" It sounded like Officer Briggs.

The tent filled with smoke.

Tied to the chair, I began hopping toward the tent door. A few feet from the door, the chair toppled over.

I was stuck.

My air ran out.

I had to take a breath.

I opened my mouth and gasped for air. It felt like I sucked a flame into my lungs.

Just then one of the Coast Guard officers ran into the tent. A bandana was tied over his face. He immediately pulled a knife from his belt and cut me free of the ropes. With his help, I stood and ran from the tent. I was gagging from the smoke. My eyes were burning.

He ran me up a slope, away from the fumes. I fell to the ground behind some rocks and fought to fill my lungs with fresh air.

"Are you okay?" he asked.

"I'm fine," I said, still panting.

"Stay here," he said and took off for camp.

Alu was there and wrapped me in a hug.

"We were so worried," she said.

I looked around the rocks at camp. A thick smoke swirled around the tents. I thought of my mom and dad.

"I have to get back down there," I said, still coughing.

"No, Wyatt!" she yelled. "Officer Briggs said to stay here. It's too dangerous!"

But, I was already running back down the hill toward the camp.

"I have to!" I yelled back. "My parents might be in there!"

With the neck of my fleece pulled up and over my mouth and nose, I sprinted past the two officers tying up the gunmen, stopped just outside the biggest tent, and cautiously looked inside.

Dr. Brezner and Officer Briggs were in a standoff, each with a gun pointed at the other. Bound to a pole at the far end of the tent, was Captain Colin. My parents were nowhere to be seen.

Dr. Brezner and the captain were coughing violently, their eyes red and watery.

Officer Briggs demanded the doctor throw down his weapon, but he would have none of it. He held out his gun, his finger on the trigger. Then, suddenly, he lost his balance and stumbled, grabbing a hold of a tent pole to keep from falling over.

Assuming the doctor couldn't see very well, I ran inside the tent toward the captain.

I assumed wrong.

The doctor turned his gun on me!

I dove for cover.

Officer Briggs made his move, charging Dr. Brezner and knocking him clean across the face with the butt of his rifle.

Dr. Brezner fell to the ground, unconscious.

The other officers ran inside the tent, guns drawn.

I knelt at the captain's side, untying him and dragging him outside. He was trembling and too dizzy to walk. Gasping for breath, he rolled onto his back, looking like he'd just had the wind knocked out of him. He couldn't talk. It took awhile, but the fresh air eventually overcame the toxins and he started to breathe easier.

"Your parents," he said, still gasping.

"Yeah," I said, anxiously. "Are they okay?"

The captain nodded.

"Dr. Brezner's men put them in a cave," he said, pointing into the forest. "Just down the hill."

I took off like a deer, running through the woods with such speed my legs could hardly keep up. At the bottom of the hill I found the cave. Scrambling up and over several rocks I made my way to the entrance. Inside the cave, it was pitch black. I couldn't see a thing.

"Mom?" I said. "Dad?"

"Wyatt?" a voice echoed through the darkness. "Is that you?"

It was Mom!

"Yes," I said, "it's me!"

"I can't tell you how good it is to hear your voice!" my mom said, her own voice trembling.

Officer Briggs and his men came into the cave waving flashlights.

"Everyone okay in here?" he asked.

"We're okay," my dad said, his teeth chattering. "Just cold and hungry."

"We'll take care of that in short order," Officer Briggs said.

I ran to my parents and hugged them as tightly as I could. Their arms were tied behind their backs, their bodies shivering.

"What are you doing here?" my dad asked, still shocked to see me.

"When we lost radio contact, Gannon insisted we come looking for you. Honestly, we thought we might never see you again."

"Where is Gannon?" my mom asked.

"The Coast Guard took him back to the ship. He had a fall and is pretty banged up, but he'll be okay."

I was fighting back tears.

"Our radios stopped working when we came ashore," my dad said, his voice still quivering. "We didn't even have time to send up a flare. We were captured before we got back to the tender. They blindfolded us, took us into the forest, and left us in this cave. We haven't seen anyone since. We thought we might never get out of here."

I hugged them again, tighter this time.

"How about untying us so we can hug you back?" my mom said.

"You got it!"

GANNON

SEPTEMBER 24
PACIFIC YELLOWFIN

Making our way to Hartley Bay, B.C.

When everyone got back to the ship my parents were hungry and dehydrated and the captain was battling fatigue and the effects of hypothermia. We sure have a long list of ailments between us, but none are life threatening, and thank goodness for that. The Coast Guard medics decided to stay on board and monitor us as Liam steers the Pacific Yellowfin to Hartley Bay, which is the nearest town with any sort of medical clinic.

Several of us have gathered in the ship's galley. It sure does feel great to all be back together again, safe and warm. Looking around, I gotta say, we sure are an unsightly bunch—everyone with pale, ghostly faces all scratched and swollen with a hundred mosquito bites apiece. I mean, it looks like a zombie convention in here or something. The only exception, of course, is Alu, who still looks as beautiful as ever.

"Shall I grab my guitar for a sing-along?" the captain said, jokingly.

We all laughed.

"Please, Captain," I said, still chuckling. "No more jokes. It hurts my ribs to laugh."

Joe brought us some hot tea and we all grabbed a mug. After dropping two sugar cubes into his cup, Captain Colin carried on.

"If my adventures as a ship captain were to continue for 100 years from this day," he said, "I would never guess that my life would be saved by a group of teenagers."

"In addition to your life," said Joe, "and quite frankly of greater importance, the rainforest itself was saved. No offense to the captain, of course."

"None taken, Joe," the captain replied with a widening smile. "A humbling statement, indeed, but quite correct."

The captain went on to explain what had happened to him and all that he had learned while held prisoner in Dr. Brezner's camp.

"The doctor had it all very well planned," he said. "Upon coming to the island, we were met by several armed men and I was immediately detained. He knew I could help with his netting operation and offered me a hefty sum of money to cooperate. Of course, I refused straightaway. That's when he ordered his men to sink the tender offshore, making it look as if the boat had capsized in the storm."

"Did he want everyone to think you were both dead?" I asked.

"That was the idea. If people thought we were dead, he would be able to continue his work undisturbed. I attempted to escape several times, but that only put me in greater danger. I believe the men were feeling compelled to do away with me sooner rather than later. That's when Wyatt and Alu showed up with the Coast Guard. Impeccable timing, I must say."

WYATT
SEPTEMBER 24, 12:46 PM
EN ROUTE TO HARTLEY BAY, B.C.
12° CELSIUS, 54° FAHRENHEIT
SKIES CLOUDY

I have to be honest, I'm having a hard time coping with all of this. It's tragic that an environmental scientist best known for his work in conservation would use his knowledge of the environment to destroy it.

"I suppose you should never underestimate what people will do for money," my dad said. "At least we stopped him before he finished the job."

The captain noticed that I was in a bad mood and did his best to cheer me up.

"The doctor did lots of noble work in his day, Wyatt," he said. "With your passion for the environment, you're just the person to pick up where he left off."

I hope one day I'll be up to the task.

"Captain Colin's right, Wyatt," my mom said. "This could be your calling."

"Maybe," Gannon said with the smirk he always has before he cracks a joke. "But your map reading skills will definitely need to improve. Hard to study the environment if you're constantly lost. Wouldn't you agree, Wyatt?"

I know he was only teasing, but if he hadn't been suffering from a concussion, I'd have stood up and smacked him one.

"I must confess," the captain said, "at the start of this journey I had serious doubts as to whether the two young gentlemen on this ship had any backbone. Now, I have no doubt. You are certainly brave explorers. Some of the bravest I have encountered."

"Truthfully," Gannon said, "we owe it all to Alu. Without her, we may have been lost on that island forever."

Alu smiled modestly.

"It's a miracle we all made it out of this one alive," my dad said.

"We definitely broke a few rules of exploration," I said.

"It goes to show you," my dad said, "just knowing the rules isn't enough. As an explorer, you have to live by them. A single slip up could cost you your life."

"The important thing is that we all made it back safe and sound," my mom said. "I think that calls for a celebration, don't you?"

Everyone agreed.

"Joe," she continued, "could we trouble you for another pot of that delicious seafood stew you made the other night?"

"Coming right up," Joe said.

Enjoying my first decent meal in days, there was one nagging question I still needed answered.

"Gannon," I said, "How did you come up with the idea to smoke out the camp with the fumes of a poisonous tree?"

"It came to me in a dream," he said, as he stuffed another spoonful of stew into his mouth.

"Come on," I said. "Tell me the truth."

"I know it may be hard for you to believe, Wyatt. But that is the truth."

I looked to Alu. A sly grin crept across her face. She leaned over and whispered in my ear.

"I told you," she said. "It was the spirits. They spoke to Gannon."

GANNON

A totem pole overlooking the harbor

By the time we arrived in port, word of our actions in the
Great Bear Rainforest had spread through the village and
the docks were lined with locals and everyone was cheering

as we came ashore. Alu jumped off the ship and ran down the dock to her parents. She kissed her mom and her father wrapped her up in his arms. After a long, loving embrace, Alu's father and uncle hoisted her onto their shoulders and carried her through the town, a hero.

As a sign of thanks, Alu's aunt gave us each a little spirit bear carved from wood and painted white. It's the perfect gift for my four-year-old cousin, Delilah, who absolutely loves bears.

"Anoogi, Tooyxsut," I said, which I'm pretty sure means, "I like it, thank you," in Gitga'tt. Alu's aunt smiled and said something back I didn't understand, so I just nodded and smiled too.

Then it was off to the medical clinic for me, where I spent a few hours getting measured for crutches, having proper x-rays run, getting my leg braced up—luckily it wasn't broken—and having good hard cast put on my arm. Tomorrow morning we're setting off for the whale research lab on Gill Island. The fact that we're all bumped, bruised, and battered doesn't matter at all to my mom. She's determined to do what she came to do, help the scientists prepare the research station for the upcoming whale migration.

But tonight was all about celebration.

The people of Hartley Bay organized a party in honor of those aboard the Pacific Yellowfin, and what a party it was, with a drum circle and traditional song and dance and a huge feast of King crab, fresh fish, potatoes, corn, boiled carrots, green beans, salad, and for dessert, a local favorite, blueberries soaked in cod oil. To be polite, I ate my entire bowl, smiling the whole time, but struggling like crazy to keep each bite down.

After dinner, Alu's grandmother spoke to the people of Hartley Bay. She's ninety-two and a highly respected tribal elder who has seen the battle for the Great Bear Rainforest intensify over her lifetime.

"There are people who want to rid the waters of fish," she said. "People who want take away the trees that stand right outside our window. People who wish to transport oil through the Great Bear. These people view the land differently. They will never understand that these actions would not only injure the soul of our people, but the soul of nature itself. Keeping the Great Bear Rainforest pristine and undisturbed, the way it was intended, this is our battle."

I honestly don't think I've ever heard a more powerful speaker. Now I know where Alu got her determined spirit.

Alu's grandmother went on.

"In appreciation of their contribution to saving this great rainforest, we would like to extend the honor of adopting Gannon and Wyatt into the Raven Clan."

Alu's grandmother gave us each a colorful native cloak decorated with an amazing totem design. In the center of the totem was the face of a spirit bear. The people of Hartley Bay applauded as the cloaks were draped over our backs and the sounds of tribal drums filled the room. We were totally humbled and made our way around the hall shaking hands and hugging everybody.

First Nation celebration in Hartley Bay

When the celebration was over, I hobbled down the path on my crutches to the pebbled shoreline. I'm seated on a rock near the marina, enjoying a moment to myself. The wooden-planked walkways that weave their way through Hartley Bay are all quiet. A red light flashes atop a spit of rocks that protects the marina from the open water. Beyond the light, a heavy fog is coming in, hiding the distant islands.

Staring into the fog on this quiet shoreline, thoughts of our adventure are jumping around in my head. I'm thinking about the incredible crew of the Pacific Yellowfin and how lucky we are to be here with them. I'm thinking about how grateful I am to have seen the spectacular wildlife that lives in this rainforest. I'm also thinking about our new friend, Alu, and the kind, strong-willed people of Hartley Bay, people who provide a voice for nature when there is none. Mostly, I'm thinking about the future of this magnificent place.

WYATT
SEPTEMBER 24, 9:12 PM
PACIFIC YELLOWFIN, ORCA CABIN
10° CELSIUS, 50° FAHRENHEIT
CLEAR SKIES

The fog has moved away. Only a few clouds hang in the sky. Again, the stars are visible. Lying here in my bed, looking out the porthole window over the water to the wild lands that surround Hartley Bay, I can't help but think of how I have been changed by this magical experience. I am a practical thinker. Always have been. But the rainforest has reshaped my thinking in many ways.

Environmentally speaking, this rainforest is of tremendous importance to us. It absorbs pollutants from the atmosphere, it gives off a great deal of oxygen and it is home to some of the most majestic and rare creatures on earth. These things are known and can be proven scientifically. But wild places like this have value far beyond the scientific.

The Great Bear Rainforest is a masterpiece of the natural world. I sound a lot like my brother here, but there is no denying, once you have experienced the power of such a place, the inspiration you get from walking into its woods, the revival of spirit you feel mingling with its wildlife, the peace you find in its silence, you will be changed. Nature on such a spectacular scale opens up your mind to endless possibilities. These things are intangible, meaning they cannot be measured physically. Still, they are very real. One thing I know for sure: I am a better person for having explored this wilderness.

For all intents and purposes, the Great Bear Rainforest is safe . . . for now. The sad truth is that it is only a matter of time before someone else goes after the forest's resources for profit. The spirit bear still needs our help. All the creatures of the rainforest need our help. The forest itself needs our help. They probably always will. What we must not forget is that we need the forest's help, too. Some would argue that our future depends on it.

Well, it's time to get some sleep. We set off for the whale research station at first light where we'll continue to do our part.

Goodnight, Great Bear, and goodnight old "spirit" of the Great Bear Rainforest.

TRAVELS WITH GANNON & WYATT'S
"FIVE LAWS OF EXPLORATION"

LAW #1
Know your destination.

LAW #2
Always maintain a healthy curiosity.

LAW #3
Make certain you are properly equipped before embarking on an adventure.

LAW #4
Document all findings.

LAW #5
Live to explore another day.

GANNON & WYATT's

North Pole

The Alaskan Arctic

Baffin Island

Denali

Kodiak Island

Cliffs of Moher, Ireland

Great Bear Rainforest

Yellowstone Park

Niagara Falls

Stonehenge

Moab   Badlands

Paris, Franc

Grand Canyon

New Orleans

Barcelona, Sp

Everglades

Bermuda Triangle

Casablanca, Moro

Tropic of Cancer

The Caribbean

Big Island, Hawaii

Galapagos Islands

The Amazon River

Machu Picchu, Peru

Tropic of Capricorn

Patagonia

TRAVEL MAP

Siberia

St. Petersburg, Russia

Moscow, Russia

Gobi Desert, Mongolia

The Great Wall of China

Himalayas, Nepal

Masada, Israel

Tibet

Cairo, Egypt

Ruins of Petra, Jordan

Persian Gulf

Taj Mahal, India

Varanasi, India

Hong Kong, China

Angkor Wat, Cambodia

The Serengeti

Kho Phi Phi, Thailand

Equator

Nairobi

Ngorongoro Crater

Okavango Delta

Bali

Darwin

Fiji

The Great Barrier Reef

Mauritius Islands

Kalahari Desert

Australian Outback

Mt. Cook, New Zealand

Cape of Good Hope

Antarctica

McMurdo Station

AUTHORS' NOTE

For tens of thousands of years, human beings existed in relative harmony with nature. It is only recently—the past few centuries—that human consumption has had a significant impact on the environment.

Though estimates vary, some researchers say that approximately 50,000 square miles of forest is lost each year. We are clear-cutting massive tracks of woodlands to make room for more development. We are consuming forests to produce building materials and consumer goods. Because of the high demand for these things, the earth's forests are at risk.

Forests give us oxygen and regulate the earth's atmosphere. Forests provide homes to over 70 percent of the world's animal and plant species. Forests allow for recreation and strengthen our connection with nature. To continue consuming the earth's forests at this rate would not just be irresponsible, it would put the future of the entire planet at risk.

Of course, we cannot expect human consumption of natural resources to stop completely. The world's population continues grow. In the year 1900 there were 1.6 billion people on the planet. Today there are seven billion. Given this reality, we need to be conscious of how we live, what we buy, the things we consume, and the impact our habits have on Mother Nature. With this in mind, we must work to reduce and ultimately offset our consumption by replenishing the forests that are so critical to our well-being.

The first and most important step is awareness. If the world's young people are aware, they will make the right choices. They will ensure that irreplaceable wilderness areas are properly managed—areas such as British Columbia's pristine Great Bear Rainforest. By considering the future, the tide will turn, and the health of the planet will be changed for the better.

Gannon and Wyatt searching for the spirit bear in the Great Bear Rainforest

MEET THE "REAL-LIFE" GANNON AND WYATT

Have you ever imagined traveling the world over? Fifteen-year-old twin brothers Gannon and Wyatt have done just that. With a flight attendant for a mom and an international businessman for a dad, the spirit of adventure has been nurtured in them since they were very young. When they got older, the globetrotting brothers had an idea—why not share with other kids all of the amazing things they've learned during their travels? The result is the book series, Travels with Gannon & Wyatt, a video web series, blog, photographs from all over the world, and much more. Furthering their mission, the brothers also founded the Youth Exploration Society (Y.E.S.), an organization of young people who are passionate about making the world a better place. Each Travels with Gannon & Wyatt book is loosely based on real-life travels. Gannon and Wyatt have actually been to Botswana and tracked rhinos on foot. They have traveled to the Great Bear Rainforest in search of the mythical spirit bear and explored the ancient tombs of Egypt. During these "research missions," the authors, along with Gannon and Wyatt, often sit around the campfire collaborating on an adventure tale that sets two young explorers on a quest for the kind of knowledge you can't get from a textbook. We hope you enjoy the novels that were inspired by these fireside chats. As Gannon and Wyatt like to say, "The world is our classroom, and we're bringing you along."

HAPPY TRAVELS!

Want to become a member of the
Youth Exploration Society
just like Gannon and Wyatt?

Check out our website. That's where you'll learn how to become a member of the Youth Exploration Society, an organization of young people, like yourself, who love to travel and are interested in world geography, cultures, and wildlife.

The website also includes:

Information about the Great Bear Rainforest, amazing photos of the spirit bear, and complete episodes of our award-winning web series shot on location with Gannon and Wyatt!

BE SURE TO CHECK IT OUT!

WWW.GANNONANDWYATT.COM

ACKNOWLEDGMENTS

We would like to offer sincere thanks to the following people for introducing us to the Great Bear Rainforest: the exceptional captain and crew of the Pacific Yellowfin, Captain Colin Griffinson, Jack, Jen, Milan, and Liam; our incredibly knowledgeable bear guide, Norm Hann; whale researchers, Janie and Hermann of Cetacea Lab; the kind and generous people of Hartley Bay, British Columbia; and Aspen Country Day and Aspen High School for continually supporting our adventures. We would also like to give a special thanks to Catherine Frank for her brilliant editorial guidance, as well as our brave travel companions Javier Kogan, Auntie Corrine, and our trusty bush pilot, Brad. Without your support, this project would not be possible. And, of course, thanks to Gannon and Wyatt for your curiosity and humor during the many hours we spent sitting in the cold and drizzly forest waiting for a spirit bear to appear.

ABOUT THE AUTHORS

PATTI WHEELER, producer of the web series Travels with Gannon & Wyatt: Off the Beaten Path, began traveling at a young age and has nurtured the spirit of adventure in her family ever since. For years it has been her goal to create children's books that instill the spirit of adventure in young people. The Youth Exploration Society and Travels with Gannon & Wyatt are the realization of her dream.

KEITH HEMSTREET is a writer, producer, and cofounder of the Youth Exploration Society. He attended Florida State University and completed his graduate studies at Appalachian State University. He lives in Aspen, Colorado, with his wife and three daughters.

Look for upcoming books and video from these and
other exciting locations:

Egypt

Greenland

Iceland

Tanzania

Ireland

The American West

If you enjoyed Gannon and Wyatt's adventure in the
Great Bear Rainforest, make sure to read the book that started it all . . .

TRAVELS WITH **GANNON & WYATT**

BOTSWANA

Nautilus Award Silver Medal Winner
Winner of Five Purple Dragonfly Book Awards
Moonbeam Children's Book Award Silver Medalist
Colorado Book Award Finalist

"Botswana has rarely had a portrayal that so accurately captures the physical
and emotional spirit of Africa . . . This is a brilliant first of what I hope will be
many books in a travel-novel series."

—*Sacramento Book Review*

"Kids with a taste for adventure will love this book, especially as told by such
engaging kids of their own age. Adults will love it too, both for the educational
nature of the story—and to fuel our own love of travel. I know I did!"

—Tracy Aiello, author, *Miracle Dogs of Portugal*

"This book is the first in what will surely become a wildly popular series that will
first fulfill and then exceed the authors' goal of instilling a spirit of exploration
in young people. Teachers and parents, alike, will love having kids reading these
books because they will help spark a love of reading in children as Gannon's and
Wyatt's venturesome accounts will keep readers on the edge of their seats!"

—Mark Zeiler, middle school language arts teacher, Orlando, Florida

MY JOURNAL NOTES

_____

_____

_____

_____

_____

_____

_____

_____

_____

_____

_____

_____

_____

_____

_____

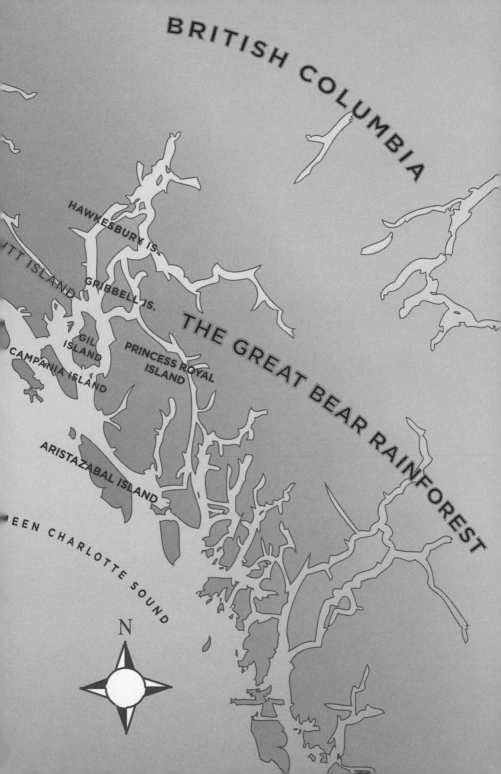

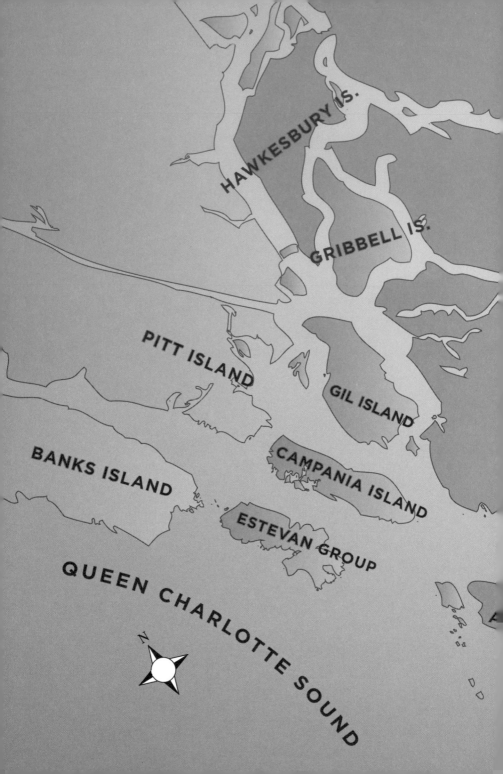